CAPITAL CITY

To Sharon

Marven Vodrey

Marven Vodrey

∞ INFINITY
PUBLISHING

ISBN 978-1-4958-0610-0 eBook
ISBN 978-1-4958-1459-4 paperback

INFINITY PUBLISHING
1094 New DeHaven Street, Suite 100
West Conshohocken, PA 19428-2713
Toll-free (877) BUY BOOK
Local Phone (610) 941-9999
Fax (610) 941-9959
Info@buybooksontheweb.com
www.buybooksontheweb.com

Table of Contents

PROLOGUE

I just got home from the hospital after a quadruple bypass surgery. I have been putting it off for a few years now and it looks like it might cost me my life. Waiting too long caused me heart problems and now I am not expected to live much longer. I have been a technical engineer for the US government for the past 30 years. I create things like their drones, robots, hovercrafts, generators and more. I started out as a scientist specializing in diseases, but that was boring. I am just lying here counting my time. Some friends still drop by, which passes the time. I am not afraid of dying. I have something else I still must accomplish, so no time is a good time. I have always believed you go to a better place from here. It gets you thinking when you hear so many things throughout your lifetime. I am religious, but being scientific, other thoughts still always come into mind, like different realities and dimensions.

The doctors told my families to all come together today, that I am getting worse. My wife and youngest daughter were crying. Everyone else was just standing there or taking turns holding one of my hands. I heard the heart monitor before I felt the pain in my chest.

CHAPTER 1   Waking up

I awoke to hear my mom call me to get up and do my work. As I looked around, I felt dumbfounded. Where was I? Looking around the room, which was a total mess, I was still in a blur as to what was going on. I recognize nothing, but yet I did. This must be a dream. I am another person. Getting up and looking in the mirror, I see myself as a young boy of 23. I knew I was 23 and I know that face and my name is Mark Anglin. I remember my other life and this new life is just now coming into focus. I took a shower and it allowed me to think who and where I am. It still felt like a dream.

"Come on Mark, I have to open the store," my mom said. I knew she had a florist in front of the house which had been in the family for three generations. I quickly ate my breakfast and did my chores for my mom, then headed for work. I worked at a cedar lumber yard. We grew and milled cedar for the Corporation. The Corporation builds their cities out of the cedar. They covered it with some coating which makes it look rich looking and fire proof. I remember in the back of my mind I would take a look at Capital City, which is about fifty miles from here.

I was driving a 1984 Blazer. It was four years old, but it got me to where I needed to go. Thinking about the time; when I was dying in bed, it was December 2017, laughing to myself. A lot of the area as for terrain was familiar, but the houses and buildings were different. This was the Killeen area, but they called it Ktown. Most of the roads here are not paved. I guess it has been fairly dry because I was kicking up a lot of dust behind me.

I had already thought about what I was supposed to do when I got to work, so I hope I had a good idea of how to handle myself. This was all new, but I seem to fall right in. The cedar camp was just ahead. Back in my days, we cut cedar down to get rid of it. Here it is being grown and produced.

"Good morning Mark", my boss said, as I entered the gate. "A little early for you", he said. I am always early, I thought, but maybe Mark was not. It is getting confusing. Hell, I don't know.

After I got off work, I help my mom with some deliveries then went to my room. It was a total mess. I cleaned everything up and got it organized. I guess Mark was not one for organization. My mom came to get me for dinner and nearly fell on her face with disbelief. "What has gotten into you", she said. "Just thought I would make some changes", I said as I headed for the door. At dinner, my mom was talking again how the corporate malls are eating up the business, that one day we will work for them.

What I want to see is Capital City. The corporate city is supposed to be 25 miles long and about 20 miles wide under a dome. The complex houses residences, businesses, and corporate offices all in one area. The tower is supposed to be 40 stories tall. I have hardly been out of the county. Most people go nowhere. There never seems to be enough money to spend traveling. Most of us really don't want to support the corporations, because they are taking over everything. So we just stay here and shop local. No matter what we do though, the Corporation seems involved.

I am just sitting here thinking about world history in school. The other entity in my mind started making comparisons. In this world, when Thomas Jefferson was elected president in 1801, he had a vision of the Silver War in the future being caused by slavery in this country. He outlawed slavery in the United States and outlying southern territories. Anyone caught buying or selling slaves would be shot. That upset the whole time slot and everything changed in history. Another happening that changed history was William Travis from South Carolina had foresight of Mexico having Texans arrested, imprisoned and saw General Santa Anna attacking Texas with his armies in 1836. Travis felt he had to do something, so he set out to help Texas. When he warned Austin of the possible upcoming event, Austin went to Mexico to complain and was arrested. Travis later with the help of Jim Bowie with his French friends and Davie Crocket with his Tennesseans could hold off Santa Anna at the Alamo outside of San Antonio until the Texas Troops and French allies from Orleans came in at about 3 AM in the morning catching Santa Anna's Troops by surprise forcing them back to Mexico. Later the Texans had all Mexican nationals sent back to Mexico creating the Texans Territory. Not long after in 1889 Texans saw where the United States might try to acquire the Oklahoma and Arkansas Territories. Texans sent troops into Oklahoma, Arkansas and New Mexico forcing local governments out and acquiring those Territories. Those territories then became a part of Texans.

The weekend came quickly. I told my mom I would be gone a few days with friends. I jumped in my car and was on my way. No one else wanted to go with me. It seemed no one else was interested in seeing the new city. The city was built over 5 years ago. It seemed the closer I got the longer it was taking. I finally got to the highway. You do not see many paved roads. I got my Blazer up to 70 MPH. That is the fastest it's ever gone. You can't drive that fast on dirt roads. Within about 20 miles from the city, I could see the tower. I go even more excited. I was now out about 5 miles and the dome was a bright orange shining in the sunlight. It was cool with the tower sticking out of the top of the dome.

Just outside the city was a large parking area. No vehicles allowed in the city. I got out of my Blazer and just stood there in awe for a moment. From what I could see of the city it seemed completely built out of the cedar. The dome that surrounded the city looked like a plastic or glass. The top of the tower of the city seemed to sit in the low hanging clouds, which made it look quite amazing. I was getting more excited as I started toward the entrance.

CHAPTER 2   The City

There were hundreds of people in line to enter the city. It looked like they are screening people before they could enter. I hope I was okay to enter. They used some kind of scanner, looking for weapons or counter band. How I knew that. I guess my split personality is kicking in. As I entered the dome and into the city, I just stopped and stared for a moment, nearly getting walked on by other people scurrying in. There were maybe 10 stores right at the entrance. All the stores looked the same except for the merchandise and colorful signs and lighting. Everything looked the same; all made out of cedar and some light metal. The boardwalk, the residences, business and everything else was made of cedar and some metal framing. It was amazing though. It looked so rich and bright. Everything seemed so perfectly clean. I just started walking. Even though everything looked the same, you just couldn't help looking at everything over and over again. I stopped to get me a sandwich, but they would not take my Texan dollars. All they took here were credits. I had to find me an exchange machine and get credits on a plastic card with my name on it.

I had walked for hours looking like the worst tourist the place ever had, laughing to myself. I thought to myself, I had better head back. It was four o'clock and it would take a while to walk back. There are no cars or taxis here. I was just about to turn around when I saw a large reservoir. There were several people sitting on bleachers and at tables watching the reservoir. Must be a rest area, I thought.

I was just about to sit at the first bleacher when I saw a girl about 20 sitting at a table about halfway up. She was just sitting there with her elbows on her knees and hands on or cheeks. I had not talked to many people since I have been here. I am a real talker. Anyways, I could not pass up talking to a very attracted lady sitting by herself. As I got closer, I could see she was wearing a green uniform like that of a nurse or medical professional. She had light brown hair and a pony tail. When I got up to her, I stood there for a moment then she looked up at me. "I am Mark", I said. "Hiii", she said like she was wondering whether to respond or not. "Would you mind if I sit with you", I said. "Not at all", she said. "I am Mandy, are you new to this district", she said. "I just came here to see what the city was all about. I have never been here before", I said. "It will be late before you get back to the entrance of the city even if you leave now", she said. "Are you a nurse", I said. "Yea, I just got off work, just sitting here waiting for the generators to start and make rainbows across the lake", she said. "I wonder why so many people were just sitting here looking at the water", I said.

About that time the generators started up and you could see the water boiling. The mist that formed made different shaped rainbows across the reservoir quit nice. "They are pretty", I said. "It is just relaxing to sit here and watch them after a long day', she said. We sat there for a few minutes not saying anything. The water was rising like a tide. Maybe it was from the heat of the generators or more water coming in from somewhere. As I was looking closer at a large pipe through the mist that came up from the water then arched back in looked like a child on it. "There is a little girl out there," Mandy yelled. I ran down to the fence separating the boardwalk from the reservoir. The little girl screamed as the large pipe shook. How did she get out there I thought. I looked around and nobody was doing anything but staring and shouting. Just then the girl fell into the rumbling water. Without even thinking about it, I took off my shoes and dove in. It was rough swimming, but I got there just as she was going under. I pulled her head up out of the water next to my cheek and started to tread water and stay afloat as long as possible. It seemed like hours, but soon the generators stopped and I could swim back to the boardwalk.

Back at the boardwalk, I placed her on her back and she yelled, so I turned her to her side. She just kept yelling. In my last life, I was not only an engineer slash scientist, but it seemed like I dealt in energy. I was able to help people with pain and cause healing to happen. She was getting a lot of pain in her right leg and lower back. I pulled her blouse up and I could see the bruised area, then I looked at the leg. Mandy said, "let me take a look." I moved to the side. "We need to get her to the hospital", she said. "Let me try something", I said.

I placed one hand on her leg and the other on her back and told the little girl to take a real deep breath. I focused on the back and leg for a few moments, and then asked her how the pain was. She said, "real bad." I touched her again and ask her to take deep breaths twice this time and I massaged her neck about six inches from the brain stem. She said, "it is feeling much better." I asked her to stand and let me touch her again. I focused on the hurt areas then told her to give me a great big hug. She just stood there and hugged me like her life depended on it for a moment. I told her then to let go and move back away from me very slowly. You could hear people all around in awe, just yammering on how I could do such a thing. The little girl finally said, "it is all gone now, thank you sir." Two security officers came up about that time and ask her name and where she lived. Mandy and I walked back up to the table not saying anything until we got to the table. "How did you do that? Are you some kind of doctor? You know that those generators could have killed you? What were you thinking jumping into the water? You could have been killed", she said excitedly. "I didn't think. No one else was going to do anything, so I just jumped in. I wasn't thinking about me, I was just worrying about the little girl", I said.

We just sat there for a while talking about energy and a little about myself, when a gentleman in an expensive suit showed up on the boardwalk. I could see people talking to him and then they pointed in our direction. He started up the steps like he was in charge. He is an intelligent looking guy with a stern face. "He must be a corporate executive or possibly the dad", she said.

He walked up and said, "you the one that pulled my daughter from the pond?" he said. Real observant, I am the only one standing around in drenched clothes. "Yes sir", I said. "You risked your life for my daughter. I am going to give you 50,000 credits", he said. "I did not help your daughter for credits", I said. "What do you want", he said. "I don't want anything", I said. "50,000 credits is probably more than you would earn in a year", he said. "I don't want anything", I said. "Well then be at my office in the morning", he said as he handed me his business card. "I don't take orders either", I said. His face then changed. "You must be an outsider", as his tone changed. "Would you please come by my office tomorrow please", he then said. "I will not be here tomorrow. I have to go home. I do not have a change of clothes nor a place to stay. Thank you anyway," I said. "What is your name young man", he said. "Mark Anglin", I said. Mandy then said, "he can sleep on my couch and I will do something about getting his clothes cleaned."

My name is Ralf Namor, and I would like to start over. I really appreciate what you did for my daughter", he said. "No problem", I said as I was shifting my wet clothes around to make them fit better. "What is your address Mandy?" I will send someone by in a little bit", Ralf said. "3002A", Mandy said. "Thank you again", he said as he hurried off.

Mandy said as she stood up heading for one of the apartments, "well, let's get you cleaned up." I followed her like a little puppy dog wondering what she had in mind. As we entered, she said, "this is my cubicle. It is not much, but it is comfortable. It is a one bedroom with a small room attached that can be used for a child, small office or storage. It has a washer dryer and a bath with tub and shower. The kitchen is small, but I don't cook for many", she said. "Why do they call it a cubicle?" I said. "All the cubicles are made somewhere else and brought here and stacked, making building the city much easier", she said.

I followed her into the bedroom. She handed me a robe and told me to get in the shower. She said she would dry my clothes and fix me a little to eat. She must have read my mind. I was getting hungry. "Want to shower with me ", I teased. "I don't think that would be a good idea", she said as she signaled me to the bathroom. I handed her my clothes through the partially open door not trying to hide anything. I have always been a big flirt. It gets me in trouble sometimes, but you never know as I smiled to myself.

I was just getting out of the shower when I heard the door knocker. I came out of the bathroom and there was a short fellow with a measuring tape around his neck. "I need to get your sizes", he said. He came over and measured it seemed like my whole body. "May I borrow your phone?" he asked Mandy. She pointed to the phone and he told someone my sizes.

"Someone will be by with a change of clothes", he said as he headed for the door. "Thank you", he said as he was leaving.

Mandy went back to the kitchen working on something to eat, stopping to put my clothes in the dryer. "They will be ready in an hour", she said. Mandy soon finished cooking and brought a plate of what looked like a type of fish with green beans and fried potato squares. It was not a lot of food, but it sure tasted good.

Soon, the door knocked again and there was a young man standing at the door. "Mr. Anglin", he said as he walked in with a whole rack of clothes, mostly suits. "May I leave these here", as he took the suits off the rack and laid them across the couch. As he was going out the door and a lady came in with two babies. "What did I miss'? she said. She handed one little girl to Mandy and came over to me, looking up and down. "Good catch", she said with a big sneaky grin on her face. "I am Melissa and this is little Carol", she said. Mandy said, "this is Tabitha, bringing the baby closer for me to get a better look. I think she was waiting to see what my reaction would be. I smiled and said a few babyish words and Tabitha smiled back. "She likes you", Mandy said. "All kids like me for some reason", I said.

"What are all the clothes for?" Melissa said. "One of the executives sent them to Mark for saving his daughter", Mandy said. "Mark huh," Melissa said. "You couldn't introduce me. I guess I need to come out of my cubicle more", Melissa said. "By the way, we usually share, right Mandy?" Melissa said. Mandy just sheepishly smiled back. "I don't know what I am going to do with all these clothes", I said.

"Well, I am off to work", Melissa said as she handed little Carol to Melissa. "Goodbye Mark", she said as she pounced out the door. "Melissa watches Tabitha in the day and I watch little Carol at night. It saves us on credits from the child care center. She works the twelve hour night shift and me the days", she said.

It was already 8 PM and dark outside. Mandy grabbed a bottle of white wine and two glasses and headed for the door. "Let's sit outside", she said as she opened the door. Outside it was like an orange glow in the sky or the dome from the artificial lighting. It was pretty and sort of romantic. "The temperature is always the same here, so you never feel hot or cold unless we have too many cloudy days and we have a problem with the solar power", she said. We just sat there for about two hours talking learning a little about each other. Finally, Mandy said we need to go in, that she had to get up at 3 AM and be at work at 4 AM. I placed my new clothes neatly on the floor as Mandy tended to the babies, making sure they were comfortable. "They will be up in a few hours", she said. I sat down on the couch and Mandy went to the bedroom and closed the door.

Just as I was about to lay my head down on the arm of the couch, Mandy opened the door and signaled me in. I wasted no time getting to the room. "Do you think you can lay next to me without keeping me up all night", she said. "I don't know. It will be really hard, but let's see what happens", I said. She smiled and got under the sheets. I was still in just the robe with nothing else on. I took off the robe and climbed in. It took about thirty minutes and Mandy scooted over and snuggled up. She seemed asleep. A few minutes past and she started slowly breathing in my ear and kissed me on the ear and the cheek. Her hand slowly went up my thigh grabbing my cock. It was like a jack in the box, solid hard. Suddenly, she was like a wild woman on top and all over me. Wow! she was great. This will be one night I won't forget.

We finally fell asleep in each other's arms. About 2 AM, one of the babies cried and then the other. I jumped up and headed for the kitchen. I put 2 bottles in water to warm them, then went to the babies when Mandy came in. "You know how to care for babies", she said. I have changed a few diapers in the past. Not for my kids but for families kids", I said. "Good to know", she said. I changed one and she changed the other. We then went back to bed after she gave me a warm kiss and shaky kind of hug.

The alarm went off an hour later. Mandy told me to just lie here a while. She went in, took a shower and came out drying her hair in different sections it seemed. She then air dried and combed her hair. She made a ponytail again but rolled it up in the back. She was dressed and heading to the door in a flash with the 2 babies in hand. "Make yourself at home", she said as she closed the door. I was still standing there nude with nothing better to do. I went back to the bed and laid down.

It seemed like only a few moments had passed and I feel someone shaking my shoulder. Looking up I see Melissa through my blurry eyes. "It's 7:30 AM, time to get moving", she said. Without even thinking about it, I threw back the sheet exposing myself. I was not used to sleeping in the nude. A sexy smile came across Melissa's face. "I have been waiting for you all morning. You know Mandy and I share everything", she said. I did not answer. I just covered up and waved for her to leave. She left the room and I got a shower and dressed. The suit I picked was blue with a heavy trim. It was smart looking. The shirt was French-cuffed. I felt like I was wearing a tux. I opened the shoe boxes. I had a pair of black, brown and gray. Man, that guy knows how to say thanks, I thought. I found something to eat in the frig and headed out the door to explore a little more before I met with Ralph Namor, whoever he is.

As I walked out the door Melissa is playing with the babies, talking baby talk to them. She looked up and said, "Wow! You must be someone really important. You know you could have come over to my cubicle after Mandy left. We could have had some fun", she said. "That would have not been respectful to Mandy. I will see you all a little later", I said." "Goodbye", she said.

Glancing at my watch as I was heading south down the boardwalk; it was nearly 9 o'clock already. I am usually up and running by 7 AM. Most of the people I passed would smile and some would say good morning, but all of them seem to think I was some important person. There were no other people out that I could see with suits on. I was getting closer to the tower now and a lot of the buildings changed. They seem to be larger and in different shapes, but all still fit together like a puzzle. I guess that is why this place is so neat; it is like someone put a puzzle together. I saw a public phone. It only took credits, but I still had credits on the card I got yesterday. I swiped it and called the number on the phone.

"Mr. Namor's office", the voice answered. "I am Mark Anglin. Mr. Namor asked if I would meet with him this morning", I said. "Hi Mr. Anglin, I am Mr. Namor's secretary, Carol. He said he would be ready for you anytime you were ready", she said. "Would you put me down for 11 AM? Oh and would you ask him if his daughter could be available. I would appreciate it", I said. "I will pass the information on Mr. Anglin. Have a great morning", she said.

Well, I have about an hour to waste. I will just walk around and see what I can get into, I thought. I wondered how long it will take to get to his office. I guess I should have asked. I stopped a man and ask him how to get to the office. He looked very surprised and sort of reluctantly told me somewhat how to get there. He had never been in that area before. It seems you have to walk everywhere here. Except for a few electric flat carts being used by service personnel, I saw no other means of transportation. This city must be slow at getting anything done. I took about 15 minutes to get to the tower. As I entered, people were scurrying all about. I saw a sign by the elevators with offices and the different floors. Executive offices are on the floor 39. Damn that is high. I hope I don't get airsick, I laughed to myself. The elevator seemed to take forever, but it is a long way up there, I thought. I just relaxed and whistled with the music playing in the elevator.

CHAPTER 3   The Governor

I am just thinking about this other personality that showed up from another place in time. It's helpful at times and others, it sort of drives me crazy. It is like my brain just won't stop thinking all the time. I dare not tell anyone. They would probably lock me up.

The door opened. The area looked much larger than the area below. I guess because it wasn't closed off. The round area was wide open. You could see offices branched off from a different section where secretaries were sitting at typewriters. Be nice if they had computers, I thought. It was actually noisy with all the typewriters all going at once. I stopped at the reception desk. "I am Mark Anglin", I said. "I have heard of you Mr. Anglin", she said with a teasing smile and flirting movements. "Go to that 5th desk over there", she said. I walked over to the desk and noticed Carol's name on the disk tab. "Hi Carol, my name is Mark", she stopped me before I could finish. "Go right in Mr. Anglin. On the door was Governor. I guess he is the top dog, I thought.

As I entered, Mr. Namor got up from his desk. "I am so glad you came Mr. Anglin. Have a seat over here", he said as he lead me to an area of nice chairs and couches. I guess his daughter heard us talking and open the door from another room. "Sit please Milea", he said. Milea not soaked look beautiful. She had beautiful long black hair and deep blue eyes. I really did not pay that much attention to what she looked like when I pulled her from the reservoir. Let's sit with Milea and then I would like to speak to you private", Mr. Namor said. "I really came here to see how Milea was. How are you doing since the accident Milea", I said. "I am doing very well thank you Mr. Anglin. Thank you for helping me", she said. May I hug you Milea. I would like you to hug me real, real hard, okay", I said. She stood up and I got on one knee. I told her to take a big breath and breathe out slowing and release me slowly. May I touch your chest and back Milea', I said. "Are you some kind of doctor", Mr. Namor said. "No, I am using energy to check her out. I can ease pain and sometimes things just go away", I said. "Please take a deep, deep breath through your nose and hold it then breathe out slowly through your mouth', I said. "How long has she had a lung condition", I said. "How can you know that, about two years now and getting worse all the time", he said with a surprising look on his face. "It feels like a growth, but not cancer. What have the doctors said about it", I asked. "There are eighteen total children in the city with the same problem. Some are worse than others. The doctors do not know what caused it, nor do they know how to treat it", he said.

I stood up and looked directly into Mr. Namor's eyes. "I would like to try something if you will allow it. This will sound kind of awkward. I need her to remove her blouse and I will remove my shirt. First, I will pinch her neck and little then hug her like before. I will then place a hand on her chest and the other in the center of her back. Please let me try it", I said. He agreed and she took off her blouse and I removed my jacket and shirt. "Please tell Carol, not to disturb us for about fifteen to twenty minutes", I said. Milea turned her back and I massaged then pinched the back about six inches from the brain stem. She turned around and we held each other for about five minutes with her taking deep breaths every so often. I then used my hands in the area of her lungs to pull the bad energy away from her. I finished up and had her put her blouse back on and I put my shirt and jacket back on. Mr. Namor, after lunch I would like to do the procedure one more time. Then I would like to you take her to the doctor and have her chest scanned", I said. "I was planning a lunch meeting, but I will cancel that and we can have lunch, and then come back to the office. How do you feel Milea", he said. "Actually dad, I feel great. I don't know what he did, but it really feels good", she said. "Can we talk for a few minutes Milea", Mr. Namor said.

Milea left the room and Mr. Namor sat back down. "Can you tell me what you did", he said. "Using the energy does not work for everyone, but I believed it did on her. It would take time to explain the process. You would probably be very satisfied with the scan results after I work on her one more time. "You're a hardheaded kind of guy, but an honorable one. I would like to offer you a job. You can have your pick of where you would like to work, maybe medical or health", he said. I appreciate the offer Mr. Namor. If I accept your offer, I may need a week before coming back. I need to go home and tell my family and let my boss know I am not coming back. He was hoping one day I would take over the cedar mill from him. I will break his heart", I said.

May I ask where you went to school", he said. "I graduated from Ktown high school and went to work at the cedar mill. Actually I have been working there since I turned sixteen. I could not afford college. I have always been somewhat smart. My mom says smart allelic. I graduated with honors", I said.

The phone rang and Carol reminded Mr. Namor to get started for lunch. Milea came out of the other room and we headed for the elevator. The door opened to a nice looking restaurant. Better than any we had back home. "This is the executive dining facility", Mr. Namor said. The attendant showed us to a table and seated Milea. He placed menus on the table and walked away. They actually had catfish on the Menu. I was in hog heaven. After the meal was served Mr. Namor asked me again where I would like to work. "Science and Technology division", I said. "Without college, do you think that might be a little over your head", he said. "No, I can handle it", I said. My other personality was reminding me of a degree in disease management and engineering. "I think you will be happy with me there", I said. He asked me about my family and told me about his. How his wife passed a few years ago and he was raising Milea alone with his super busy schedule.

After lunch, we went back to his office and I spent about 20 minutes with Milea. I then asked Mr. Namor to call medical and make sure they could do a scan today. About 2 PM, we headed for the hospital. It took about forty minutes to walk there. "It takes a long time to get around this city", I said. "We do not allow any gas vehicles in the city and the electric is saved mostly for service", he said. My mind popped again. I was thinking of all the things I could make that would benefit this city. My split personality kicked in again.

We entered the hospital and a technician was standing by to take Milea for a scan. Mr. Namor and I sat there for a few moments talking until Doctor Revis came up. "How are you Ralf", he said. He sounded like an old country doctor. "This is Mr. Anglin", Mr. Namor said. "It's a pleasure", he said.

The technician came out and asked the doctor to look at the results all puzzled. After about five minutes, he came out with a picture of the scan in hand. "I don't know how it is possible, but the growth has entirely disappeared. What did you do, or she do, or, stuttering", he said. Mr. Anglin did it with energy", he said. "I have heard of people healing with energy, but never seen any results. Mr. Anglin, this is amazing. Would you think about looking at the other seventeen children with the same affliction", he said. "I would be happy to Doc, but I want you to know, it does not work on everyone. I will do my best to help the children", I said. The doctor walked away shaking his head and mumbling. A few minutes later Milea and the technician came out. She was laughing loud and yelling she was well. "Thank you, thank you, Mr. Anglin", she said. "Please call me Mark", I said. "Daddy, I'm well, I'm well", she kept saying.

On the way back to the office, I explained to Mr. Namor and Milea that she could have severe pain in the area of recovery six to eight hours after recovery. You need not call the doctor. Just give her some medicine and try to get her to sleep. She will be fine in the morning. I gave him Mandy's phone number and ask him to call me if he wanted me to come over. I did not care what time it was, just call. Before leaving, he gave me a bank card with 5,000 credits on it, saying it was an advance on my new job.

It was after 5 PM before I got back to Mandy's. She was outside with the babies. Melissa probably already went to work. "Hi Mark, I wondered if you were coming back", she said as she placed little Carol in her baby carrier. She wrapped her arms around my neck and pecked around my face first, then gave me a warm kiss. I did not realize it, but I missed her today. Mandy really is a warm person. "I am sorry I had to work this weekend. They were short of help," she said.

"Let me fix you something to eat Mark", she said. "I would love whatever you make", I said, thinking about the catfish lunch. She fixed some kind of thin beef with vegetables and fruit. It was very good. Mandy had to stop a few times to pay attention to the babies. "We can stay up later tonight. I have the next 3 days off", she said. We stayed up to about 10:30 PM talking about her day and mine. I did not mention the healing though. I then told her I was leaving in the morning and would not be back until the following Saturday. "I was hoping to have three days together", she said. I told her I was sorry and why I had to go back home. We went to bed about 11:30PM and I swear we were up all night making love unless the babies were crying. She acted like she had not had sex in years.

The next morning I dressed in my old clothes. Mandy fixed breakfast and I headed out the door after she hung on me for quite a while, I guess hoping I would stay. It took me about two hours to get to the entrance. I exchange $2,500 Texans dollars and then headed out to my vehicle. It felt good to be out of the city. I don't know why. Maybe it's just that I was going home. Being under the dome makes you feel like you are inside all the time.

CHAPTER 4   Going Home

We haven't had rain for a few months now. We are about due. Everything is so dusty. The cedars grow well this time of year and the mill is probably still going full speed. The Desert Willow trees are pretty right now in all colors. The trees keep the dry landscape looking spring like. I see the Ktown road coming up. I sure hate the dirt roads after driving on blacktop. The dust quickly billowed up behind me as I hit the road. I had already rolled the windows up and put on the air. It took about another forty minutes and I was pulling up to the drive. I always say I hate this place, but it sure fills good to be home.

I went into the flower shop. Mom was working hard as usual. There were two ladies looking around. I walked to the back and picked up things and cleaning. I never have been one to sit on my hands. Mom finally came back and sat down taking a deep breath. "I don't know what we would do if this property had not already been paid off. It is getting harder and harder every day Mark. How was your trip", she said nearly all in one breath. You may or may not like what I will tell you. I told her the story of the last 2 days. While talking, I noticed her face changing. Because of my split personality now, I say things differently, I know things I never knew before and my actions seem to switch back and forth between me and my other me. "Where did you learn all this stuff", she asked. "I don't know, I guess I picked it up here and there", I said. I left out the part about the $2,500. I pulled the cash from my pocket and handed her $2,000. Her eyes lit up. She said something and the words did not seem to come out. She stammered for a moment. Before she could get the words out, I told her how I got it. Mom told me she needed to finish up and she would talk in a while. She closed at 1PM on Sunday. Back in the old days she was only opened 5 days a week and only work weekends for special occasions.

I went to my room and laid on the bed. My head thought again about all the things I could do. Some of the things I thought about, I did not even know what they were or meant. I sure hope I can get my head together soon, I thought. I dozed off for a while and I opened my eyes just as my mom entered the room slapping the money against her hand. "Does this mean you are actually considering working for the corporate people", she said. "Actually mom, I am excited to work for them. You would not believe the technology they have and how nice everything seems there. I know you hate the corporations because they are slowly taking over everything, but there is a lot of good there also", I said. It will take a while to change her mind about them, I thought. "How much are they going to pay you Mark," she said. "You know, I don't know, I just did think to ask at the time", I said. "I hope it is more than they pay at the mill plus your extra side jobs. $2,000", she said as she walked away and out of the room. With my full- time and part-time jobs, I make about $3,000. I have money in my pocket now and still haven't started. In my mind, it is telling me 100,000 credits a year is what I need. I am going nuts. It's like I am talking and carrying on conversations with myself.

I thought about Milea and those other children. I need to get a biopsy of the children and test it in a Spectrometer and see what is in the tissue. Maybe then I can figure out what is causing the growth. I wonder if they have a Spectrometer. They did in 2017, I thought. I wish I could get my two brains working together so I don't surprise myself. Be nice if I could come up with a cure. I am sure there are probably more than just those few children with the same growth.

I could smell chicken cooking, so I got up headed for the kitchen. I was pretty hungry. She made chicken, squash and fruit. My mom did not believe in starchy foods. As soon as I put the first bite in my mouth, my mom questioned me. It was awkward answering because of the other thoughts in my mind. I just took my time and thought before opening my mouth. "Could we possibly answer questions later, the food is getting cold", I said. She got a whipped child look on her face and just sat there for a moment. "I will speak with you later", she said as she got up from the table.

After lunch, I fed the chickens and watered the trees and shrubs in the nursery. Chuck my dog appeared from down the road, probably after hanging out with some female. He ran with tail wagging like he had not seen me in quite a while. I petted him for a while and then went into the shop to finish cleaning up, so it will be ready for the morning. Mom came in saying nothing and made large bows. There must be a funeral tomorrow, I thought.

That evening when I went to lie down, I thought about how they have no way of getting around the city other than walking. What if there was an emergency like a fire, some lady having a baby or someone needing medical attention for a life-threatening injury. I know so many things that can help people. Lying there, I get more excited with every thought thinking of all the inventions I could come up with. I know they were invented by someone else, but I would get credit for it, I smiled.

The alarm went off at 6 AM. I guess I fell asleep with my clothes on. I hurriedly got up and took a quick shower and got dressed. Mom got up about 6:45 AM and headed for the shower. I made the coffee which I have never done before, fixed me some toast and boiled eggs and was out the door. I had to be at work by 8 AM but was always at least fifteen minutes early. Jordan, my boss, would always say when I entered the gate I am a little early and always when leaving, that one day I will run this mill. On the way to work, I was thinking about how I would tell Jordan I would work for the "man." He did not like the corporation, because they told him how to run his business, but he made a great deal of money from them. Jordan was probably one of the richest men in town.

As I entered the gate, Jordan was standing there as usual waiting the crews to show up. "Good morning Mark. A little early for you isn't", my boss said. This time I pulled in next to his office shack. "When you get a moment Jordan, I need to speak with you", I said as I was getting out of my Bronco. I usually pull in next to the saw mill and go right to work. I saw him scratching his head. About twenty minutes had passed and Jordan started towards the shack.

"What's going on", he said as he opened the shack door. Stepping inside, he already had the swamp cooler going to cool things down. It was already about eighty degrees outside. I need to give you notice, but it will only be one week instead of two", I said. "You going to work for another mill", he angrily replied. "No, I am going to work for Capital City", I said, sitting uneasy at the moment. "I will give you a raise if you stay on", he said. "No, I really would like trying to work for them Jordan. There are a lot of opportunities for something new in my life", I said. "You have a great future here Mark. Corporate is talking about starting a new city soon and adding on to the older ones. That means a lot of cedar. I am looking at nearly doubling what we do now", he said. "Jordan, you have always been good to me and I really have enjoyed working here, but I just want to try something new", I said. Actually if I was still just Mark, I probably would never even think about going anywhere else. "Okay Mark, you know you always have a place here. I hate to lose the best worker I have ever had. You never complain and always work extra hours and weekends when asked. Actually I never ask, you always know exactly what to do", he said.

The rest of the week went about the same. Jordan leased another 5,000 acres from one of the ranchers to increase production. I may have been working a little slower because my head was always day dreaming of new things I could accomplish. It was like I had already done it before and I may have, I thought. On Friday, I told most of the guys good luck and thanked Jordan again. He handed me my weekly 500 dollar check and wished me good luck.

That night my mom was complaining a little about what she would do without me. I told her I would check back from time to time. My mom never remarried after my dad died. She really is an attractive lady and takes good care of herself. She just feels old and that no one wants an old lady. I try to reassure her how nice she looks and what she is like all the time, but she just says thank you, it just because you are my son you think that way.

I set the alarm for 5 AM. I wanted to get to the city early. I never found out where I am supposed to live, besides how much I would make. I showered, got dressed and headed out. It had been cloudy for a few days and it rained last night. The roads won't be dusty, but I could feel every hole in the road until I hit the blacktop.

CHAPTER 5   First Day At Work

I got to the city about 7 AM. At the entrance, everything was dark. People were lined up all the way out in the rain. Some had umbrellas and raincoats. When I finally got up to the gate, I was drenched. I thought I would look about the same as the last time I was here with a smile. "What happened to the lights", I asked the security guard. "Whenever we have no sunlight for a few days, this side of the city has no lights. Everything runs off of solar energy. Until the sun comes out, we are without power. The water generators only take care of the main part of the city", he said. I thanked him and went on my way.

This was no way like the last time I was here. It was not bright and the stores were closed. After walking about ten miles it was lighting up some, but more like evenings than the day. My mind thought about generators and other things while walking. I headed for the tower suitcases in hand. The elevator was slow with the absence of power. I thought I would never get up. When the elevator door finally open and I mean really slowly, I ventured into the corporate area. The receptionist remembered my name, saying good morning. A few other ladies and one man said good morning as I headed for Carol's desk.

"Good morning Mr. Anglin, I have been expecting you", she said reaching down into a drawer for a piece of paper, some keys and then two more pieces of paper that look like notes. "This is your keys to your cubicle. No one locks their doors around here, but your keys anyway. This is your address, 2517B, do you need directions?" she asked. "I think I can find it, thank you", I replied. Here is a message from Mr. Namor, one from the doctor at medical and one from the director of Science and Technology", she said. I read the note from Mr. Namor first. He was thanking me for coming to work for him and that if I needed anything contact Carol or Gerald Wright he would be at corporate in Antonio for a few days. The other note was from Ryan Adams and said to please see him upon arrival. The doctor also wanted to see me. It was probably about the children.

"Carol, where may I find Mr. Wright", I asked. "See Judy over there", she said. "Thank you", I said. I then moved over to see Judy. "Hi Judy", she stopped me before finishing. "Hi Mr. Anglin, what can I do for you", she said. "I would like to speak to Mr. Wright if he is available", I said. Wow! Thinking to myself, does everyone know who I am? Judy picked up the phone and told Mr. Wright I need to speak to him. A few seconds later, the door open and Mr. Wright stood there with a big smile on his face. "I have heard a lot of good things about you Mr. Anglin", he said. "I don't know what I did to get so much attention", I said. "I need to speak with you about some really important matters. It could take a while", I said. "I will take whatever time you need Mr. Anglin. I have been expecting you", he said.

We went into the office and he showed me to the lounge area. I ask if we may sit at his desk, so we moved over there. I probably should see Mr. Adams first about what I will ask you, but I needed to meet you anyways", I said. "It's okay, how can I help you", he said. "What I am going to ask will probably cost and may need your approval or approval by the corporation. Would you please hand me a sheet of paper and pencil please", I said. I drew out a somewhat picture of a generator. I then told him basically how the machine would work. I told him I would need a shop to work in and a person with electrical and mechanical experience to be assigned to me if possible. Not only that but I needed to make a new metal made of graphite and aluminum I call graphluminum. I would need someone to help me build a platform to form the new material, so maybe someone in manufacturing. Probably the most expensive part of the machine would be the magnets and creating the new metal.

Mr. Wright was not a technical person and I had to answer the same questions differently to help him somewhat understand what I was telling him. After about 45 minutes he said, "something like that would mainstream the corporation to a new level. Are you sure you can build this thing?" "I am positive I can build it if I can get the materials and help I need", I said. "You know Mr. Anglin, I have heard some great things about you, but nothing on the level you are talking about. You will get everything you need as fast as we can get everything together for you. I will tell Judy to get a hold of Kelly, Director of Manufacturing and Bryan, Director of Science and Technology and anyone else you want and make this happen" he said. He picked up the phone and told Judy what to do. It seemed like just a few moments later and Bryan was knocking on the door. He must have been around the office somewhere. "What's all the fuss?" he said as he was walking in. "Take a look at this", Mr. Wright said. "Okay, what is it", he said. "You tell him Mr. Anglin", Mr. Wright said. "First, let me say, would you please just call me Mark", I said. "Okay", they said. "This is a magnetic perpetual generator. Once started with a nine volt battery, it will run buy itself. I need to build a working unit first, and then manufacturing can make a larger scale. Because I do not know how much energy this complex actually uses, I am not sure how many units it would take for each area or the city. It could be wired into your solar and come on when energy is low, run along with the solar power or run on its own. Bryan, if I may call you Bryan. I would also like to create a new alloy metal that will be about as thin as a thick piece of paper to about a quarter an inch and be as strong as five inches of solid steel", I said.

Bryan was sitting there looking confused. "Where did you go to college and what was your degree", he said. I had to stop for a moment and remember who I was. "I could never afford to go to college Bryan", I said. "Where did you work before coming here", he said. "At a cedar mill", I said. "How is it you believe you can build a machine like this? When Mr. Namor told me you were coming over to my division and how little he knew about you other than helping his daughter, I had negative thoughts about you. I still have negative thoughts about you", he said. "I will tell you this Ryan, the most expensive and hardest part of the generator is the metal covering. I can build a working model fairly quickly if the magnets I need are readily available. Then you can make a decision of what you think about me. If I do not succeed, I will not stay here. I will go on home with my tail between my legs", I smiled. "You sound pretty sure of yourself. Tell me what kind of magnets you need and if I have them, you can start anytime. I will make an area and have the materials you need", he said. "That is all I ask", I said standing up and shaking his hand. Ryan, see if you can find me a level 5 or 6 stand-alone magnets. They do not have to be large. "You seem much older than what you are", he commented as he was leaving.

"I don't know who you are Mark, but I am impressed. Please let me know how everything is going and if you need anything else", Mr. Wright said. He showed me to the door and as I was leaving Judy said Carol needed to see me again. I scurried over to Carol's desk. "I forgot to give you your employee card. You need to remember your employee number to get around. It is 1028832. You will need this to enter certain areas of the city and it collects your pay credits each week. Also, Doctor Roberts wants to have lunch with you if you are available", she said. 'Would you dial him for me", I asked. "No problem", she replied. I arranged to meet Doctor Roberts in the executive dining hall.

By the time I got to the dining hall it was just past 11:30 AM. Doctor Roberts had not gotten there yet, so I got a table. The receptionist remembered me with the Governor and seated me right away thinking I was someone real important. I ordered a cup of coffee and about 15 minutes later the doctor came in. "How are you Mr. Anglin", he said. "Please call me Mark", I asked. "Okay Mark, what looks good", he said. "I love catfish", I said "That looks good", let's get two plates he told the waiter. "I guess you know why I want to talk with you Mark", he said. "Yes Doc and I have a few things for you. First I need to ask you if you have what I call a spectrometer or some way to find out the chemical breakdown of the biopsies. If I can find out what the chemical makeup is, then I could possible find out what is causing the growths and come up with a cure. I have notice a good number of people that cough around here. I am willing to bet if you tested more people including adults, you will find the infection is worse than you think", I said. "Where did you graduate from", he asked. "I only went to high school", I responded. "How is it you know so much without the knowledge", he asked. "I have always been smart and I read a great deal. My family could not afford for me to go to college", I said. "You must read a lot", he said. "I don't have a spectrometer, but science and technology does", he said. "Doc, I am working on a project right now that is nearly as important as yours. If you can give me access to the biopsies, I will try to work it in even if it is at night", I said. "I will get you access to all medical on your card so you can come anytime. If you need any help, I will try to be at your service or get someone to help you Mark."

After lunch, I walked back over to the science and technology building. It was large with a lot of very big cubicles and it went up about six floors. I entered where it said technology and used my card key to enter the door without ringing the bell. As I entered, a mousy looking, tight-faced lady jumped up and wanted to know what I needed. Maybe she did not get the word I was coming. "I am Mark Anglin and I will be working here temporarily. Where am I supposed to work?" I said. "We have an office over here for you Mr. Anglin", she said escorting me to the side of the large room where there were about fifty people working at different stations. "This will not do", I said. I could hear a lady off to the side say, "what does he want, a suite?" Are you the area manager her Miss" waiting for her answer. "I am Jodi Roberts", she said. "Jodi, would you get a pen and paper? I need you to write down items I will need by tomorrow morning", I said. She ran back to her station for a notebook and returned the same way. "Yes sir", she said. "First, I need an area of about fifteen foot square minimum to work out of. I need a drafting table with plenty of drafting paper and pencils, pens and different shade markers. A stool for the table would be nice. I need a metal table at least four foot long and three foot wide, chair to match the table, at least four table clamps with spreader, assorted screws, nails, large roll of number 11 copper wire, 24 of heavy duty electrical wiring, and 20 foot of 120 volt electrical wire, one inch by twenty four inch solid steel polish still round bar, two electrical button switches, two flip switches, one 120 volt 3 prong plug, four six square inch by quarter inch metal plating, two four foot by two foot by quarter inch pieces pliable sheets of plastic, assorted screwdrivers, hammers, and wrenches and finally an arc welder with accessories" I said. "Who is this guy", some person said. "I don't know", another person said. "What is plastic", Jodi asked.

"Forget that", I said. They don't have plastic here yet, I thought to myself.

"Now I need you to find me a person who knows somewhat about electricity and can handle machinery. It would be nice if the person knows that they would probably have to work some major hours over a few days" I said as I was looking around the area for a place to work. "I have a girl that has the experience and I believe willing to work the hours you need. She is also a hard worker and go-getter", Jodi said. "Can you have her and all the materials that I ask for here by nine in the morning? I will run late in the morning. I will work most of the night in medical I believe", I said. "I will get people working on it right away sir", Jodi said. "Jodi, please do me a favor and smile. You will look at lot prettier and feel a whole lot better", I said. Jodi squeezed out a smile.   "Now Jodi, I need to know where I can find a spectrometer." I said. "Does anyone know what a spectrometer is?" Jodi yelled out. "You will need to go to the science area for that", a voice yelled back. "Go out the door, turn left, go down to the bottom floor and walk for about twenty minutes and you will see the sign", Jodi said. I looked at my watch, thanked Jodi and was out the door. Damn time goes fast. I hurriedly walked to the science department in about fifteen minutes.

I used my card to open the door. "I am Rhonda, may I help you", a lady said as I entered. "I am Mark Anglin are you the area manager." "I thought you were going to be working in technology", she said. "I believe I will be working in a lot of places in the city." I need to find a spectrometer and someone to help me a little", I said. I followed Rhonda over to a lady working at a microscope section. "Judy, would you please help this gentleman with one of the Spectrometers", Rhonda said. When Judy turned around I nearly dropped my jaw. "You are absolutely beautiful. If you are half as smart, I would love working with you", I said. "I have two doctor degrees and graduated at the top of my class", she said. "I love an intelligent lady. I need a spectrometer that can tell me what the makeup is of a biopsy from a young lady's lung", I said. "Are you a doctor? We have been working on that same disease off and on for over 6 months now", she said. "No, I am not a doctor and I would like to see your journals on that disease by this evening if possible. Have you gotten anywhere with it at all?" I said. "Do they think one person is going to do what twelve others were not able", she said. "I don't know Judy, maybe with what you have in the journals and my findings; maybe we can come up with something. A voice from across the room, asking if I was the person that saved the little girl at the pond. "Yes I was," I said. Judy took me over to the spectrometer. "This is the one that you will need", she said. "It's kind of old isn't?" I said. It is brand new model and it just came out. Have you seen a newer version?" she asked. I changed the subject real fast. I keep forgetting these people are twenty years behind me. Rhonda, would it be possible to come here late at night and work?" I asked. "You have been upgraded to a level nine clearance Mr. Anglin. You can go nearly anywhere in the city without asking", she said.

"Who do you know in corporate to give you a level nine Judy said? I only have a level seven and the Governor is a level nine", Judy said. "Judy, may I ask if you were to be free to work some nights on this medical project. I would really appreciate it. I am also working on another project over in technology that I need to finish as soon as possible", I said. "If you look around in the evening, you will see a lot of us working on projects. We get started and it's hard to stop. I will work with you Mr. Anglin", she said. "Please call me Mark", I said. "Very well Mark", she said. I said goodbye and left the area. On the way back I stopped and asked Jodi to get me a telephone and two sets of coveralls for a six foot guy, and then I headed for my cubicle.

I was nearly at my cubicle. Damn I hate that reference. They need to call them apartments, I thought. I then remembered my other clothes at Mandy's. I opened the door not even paying attention to what is was like and place the clothes I brought from home in the door and headed to Mandy's. It was getting close to 5 PM. I should have called. When I got to the reservoir, I did not see Mandy, so I headed up the stairs to her cubicle. I was just about to knock when she opened the door. She wrapped her arms around me and hugged for what seemed like a long time. "Miss me?" I said. Mandy made us some sandwiches for dinner. "I have got to go to work tonight Mandy", I said. "No, no", she said. "I would like to ask Doctor Roberts to let you help me on a project I am working on, if you want", I said. "I will do anything with you Mark", she said. "I am going to try and find out what is causing the lung disease in the children. I have another lady in science that will also be working with us. I will be going by medical tonight to pick up samples of the biopsies and take them over to science to begin working. I will be working a lot of hours until these two projects are done and then maybe we can spend some time together. By the way my cubicle, I would rather call it a residence or an apartment, is 2517B. Do you have a small jar or something that I can use for a water sample?" I said. "I have some bottles the baby food comes in", she said. We talked for a few moments and I gathered up my clothes and left for my apartment. That sounds better, doesn't it?" I thought. On the way, I stopped and got a water sample from the reservoir. When I got to the apartment, I just threw my things down and laid across the bed.

CHAPTER 6 Lung Disease

I did not realize how tired I was. I looked at my watch as I was sitting up and saw it was already 8:40 PM. I have to get moving. I didn't change clothes, just jumped up and out the door. When I got to the medical center, all the doors were locked. I put my card in the slot and keyed in my number and went on in. A nurse at the emergency reception said Doctor Roberts had already gone for the day, but that you could go on to the lab and she pointing the way. A technician in the lab helped me find the biopsies. I gathered up 5 of the most recent biopsies. The containers had the girl's names, date of biopsy and where they lived. Perfect, I thought. They also had blood samples from each child. This will get me started. I had already in my mind what might cause the growth. After the test tomorrow, I will find out if I am right or not.

It took a while to get over to the science building. It seemed darker than usual tonight. I guess maybe for the lack of power, I thought. By the time I got there, it was after 10:30 PM. There were four people in there slaving over their microscopes. I saw Judy's area. On the desk were a bunch of journals opened up to different pages. I sat down on her stool and started reading. I had just finished reading the first one when Judy can in. "I had to get me something to eat. Where do you want to start?" she said. "I only read a portion of this one journal and it said the sample was normal. How could a growth be normal?" I asked. "It could be normal for what that person was looking for, I don't know", she said. "I brought five tissue samples and some water that we can get started with", I said. "Let's forget the journals. I re-read them and could not find anything of value. Let's, start with this one and see what it looks like. I do not know if any of these tissue samples have been read on this new spectrometer." It will take about twenty minutes per sample", she said. While she started the first sample, I put some of the water from the reservoir on a slide and focused in. In my other life, I have a research background, so it was like walking for me. At first I saw nothing. Then I doubled the magnitude and I could see differently little things moving around. I strengthen the magnification to get a better look. Everything looked normal except an orange looking possibly bacteria. The orange object seemed to have a large and small tail that attached itself to the something. They activated as soon as the slide got warm from the light. Watching the orange object move around and then try to attach itself to other objects in the water made it look like it was feeding. This was not bacteria as I know it. This was something I have never seen before. I watched it a little longer and it seemed to attach itself to another object in the water, and then changed color to green. A light went off in my head. "An algae", I yelled. One other technician asked me to quiet down. "Judy, look", I said. Judy came over and looked at the slide. She saw the same thing happen to another object. "Where is this sample from?" she asked. "I brought it from the reservoir on the east side", I said. She watched it again, changing the magnitude back and forth. "It is sort of like a copepod. It is feeding on objects in the water", she said. "Did any of them turn green?" I asked. Yes", she said. "While you are running the other samples I am going to go get something and be right back", I said.

I nearly ran out the door and across to the dining facility. I got permission to go to the back from the manager. I asked one of the employees if he could cut me a small slice of pork, beef and the breast of chicken. I told him I was working on a disease in the lab and needed it for a test. He gave me a nice piece of each and I headed back to the lab. When I got back, Judy had the first results ready and already started another. Looking at a tissue with a spectrometer shows all the different entities in different colors. We figured out all the entities except one that was green and red/green and orange. Judy said green and orange. So we went with that. "You look and act like a real scientist", Judy said. I need a flat glass container with a screened top", I said. She handed me a container and I placed slices of the three meats in different corners and put the screen on top. "Can we put this in a place that is about 98.6 degrees for a few days", I asked. Judy went over to a cabinet and brought back a medal box and plugged it in. She set the temperature and set the container inside.

"What are you brainstorming", Judy asked. "I am going to lay it out what I feel, think and what we should do. Just let me know what you think. Maybe you should write some of this in a journal", I said. We had not even started a journal yet. I am falling down on the job again. Judy left the first couple of pages blank and wrote. "First of all looking at the addresses on the biopsies, all those children live in the 3000 area of the city. That is the east side closes the reservoir. When I jumped into the water to save that girl the other day, the water had so much chlorine I thought I would turn white all over. It was sickening. The bubble that surrounds the city has an orange tint. I do not know what it comprises yet. Maybe that is where the orange color comes from. People go out to watch the rainbows every afternoon when the generators start up that are caused when the mist is thrown in the air. I think a of chemical reaction was formed in the water causing the problem and is carried by the mist and we breathe it in. I will request blood samples for a child and an adult from the east and west to compare them. We have blood samples of the infected children. I will bet that the algae or whatever it shows up in the blood and the biopsies and all except the samples of blood from the east. I do not know how it could be algae though. The chlorine should kill all algae bacteria. It could have produced a different stain. We need to run spectrometer on all samples and see if we can come to an intelligent conclusion", I said sitting down.

"You tried to get that all out in one breath, didn't you? I am impressed. We have been working on this thing forever and you come up with a possible solution in one night. I think I love you", she said. We both sat there for a moment saying nothing until the spectrometer stopped. Judy went over to put another sample in. "Those samples of meat have been treated with the water. I want to see what they look like in a few days. In the meantime let's play with more samples of meat while we are waiting. Judy cut a slice of beef and I a slice of chicken. It was hard trying to get a thin slice of chicken. We both put our samples under microscopes and touched the water to them. I could only see seven of those little orange things and they all dove at the meat once the water touched the meat. Judy and I were both logging all that we had seen. "This is incredible. Look at how fast they feed. And as soon as they feed, they start multiplying", she said. "This is like a really bad virus. I think they are attacking because the meat is unhealthy, already dead. Those children affected must have been unhealthy at the time the growth started", I said.

"Judy, after we run the last test, let's tidy up and say goodnight. I have an early day tomorrow on another project. Please work with whatever we have and journal everything. I will have Mandy or someone at medical to get you the other biopsies and blood samples. You can start working on those until I get back if you will. You could also have the nurse get you anything else you may need from medical", I said.

After a few moments later, I gave Judy one of those power hugs and headed to the apartment. I was beat. I don't think I got this tired splitting wood. I opened the door and went in. On the table were a basket and a note. "Enjoy your new home. The fruit is really good for you and it makes the home smell better", signed Carol. She is such a sweet lady, I thought. I laid down without taking a shower.

The alarm went off at 6 AM and I surprisingly got up easily and headed for the shower. I went over to the executive dinner and had breakfast then headed to the science and technology building. Jodi had a smile on her face as she wished me good morning. "Thought you were going to be late", she said. I went back to my corner and it looked like everything I ordered was there. About a quarter to eight, a cute little blond girl came in with coveralls on. Jodi pointed over at me. I guess that is Sunshine, I thought. "Hi, I am Sunshine", she says walking up and noticing me glancing up. "I am Mark. I heard you were the best darn worker around these parts", I said. "I will do my best", she said. "We are going to build a generator. I would like to keep what it actually is confidential until it is done if possible. We need to put it together as fast as possible. I just don't want a bunch of people standing over us asking the same questions and stopping us from work", I said. "You got it boss", she said. "I will draft up a somewhat blueprint for you to follow along as we work. Have you ever worked on an electric generator before", I said. "One gas powered and one all electric", she said. "I have built one of these before, but it has been awhile. The hardest part is getting the magnets in the right places. The magnets are not numbered. I hope they are strong enough", I said. I stop for a moment and put on the coveralls provided. Sunshine went right to work. She just might work out fine. This project will put a feather in my cap, I thought. I am really not much for hype, but I need this for leverage.

About 9 AM, Judy called the managers number. Jodi yelled over to me. "Thank you, Jodi", I said. "Your phone will be hooked up sometime today", Jodi said. "I got a hold of Doctor Roberts and Mandy. They said they will try to have all that you have asked for by 1PM if that is alright. Mandy said she will get the biopsy samples to me this morning so I can get started. Is there anything else you need Mark", Judy said. "No, I appreciate all that you are doing Judy", I said. "By the way, is Mandy your girlfriend?" she asked. "She is a very nice lady that I met when I first came to the city and she has helped me a lot. We are not dating, but yes, I do like her a lot", I said. "What time are you coming over", she said. "I will try to be there after lunch", I said as I hung up. "Thank you, Jodi for getting all these things together me. It will make it much easier to get this project completed. I owe you", I said. "No problem Mr. Anglin", she said. "Mark", I said. "Mark", she said as I walked back to my corner.

Sunshine was a little hellfire. She was really getting to work. She already had the coil nearly wrapped by the time I got back over. "This thing going to run on a nine volt battery", she said with a smirk. "You know your electricity. What if I told you that the battery is just to start the generator and then it would run all by itself", I said. "You're crazy, but I will get it done for your Mark. What are the magnets for", she asked? "That is what is going to make the generator self-perpetual", I said. "Um", she murmured. While you are working on that, I need to get to work on the pads", I said. "I don't see how rubber is going to last long. That rod will eat right through it", she said. "It is not rubber. It is a graphite alloy, I said. I brought a small Teflon frying pan from the apartment. They were nice enough to furnish me one I thought. Sunshine was shaking her head when she saw me scoring the pan with a chisel. I hope this Teflon is strong enough to support the heat I will put it through. I had a large box of graphite and some foil I picked up. I poured the graphite powder in first and then set the foil on top. It seemed to melt right in. I had to use a glove to pick up the frying pan. The aluminum around the metal shaft of the pan just fell off. I shifted it back and forth then took it off the heat. I then sprayed it with C02 and it turned a rusty color as though it had been oxidized. I waited a minute and dumped it out. The C02 shrunk the alloy to allow it to come out of the scored groves. "Sunshine, take a look", I said. "It looks and feels like a rubber, but different", she said. "It is a graphite aluminum alloy that I call graphluminum. This one piece is at least as strong as an inch or more piece of solid steel. It is pliable and is flameproof to twelve hundred degrees", I said. Amazing, I could think of a hundred things to use that for", she said.

I rolled the arc welder into place and put one of the clamps on the metal table and attached the alloy. "You can't cut this thing with scissors or heavy cutters. You need an arc welder with high temperature", I said. As I was cutting, Sunshine watched with amazement. She had the biggest smile on her face. "I am going to learn a lot from you today Mark. Where have you been all my life", she said. When I got finished with the two pieces, I then placed a rod in the clamp and held the rod to the center of the alloy and used the ark welder and just barely going around the middle making the alloy for a light cone surface. I then pierced the alloy along the sides with six holes each. You can't just poke holes in this stuff. "Amazing", Sunshine said.

"I am going to a dining facility and get us some sandwiches for lunch if that is okay. I would like to get this model finished by early afternoon", I said. "Okay boss", she said. I went over to the executive dining facility. The receptionist was going to seat me, but I just ask for Peter the waiter. Peter can over and I placed the order with him and sat in the chair and waited. When he returned, I asked "let me ask you something. How do you leave a tip?" I asked. "They generally don't tip here", he said. "How do I leave a tip with these credits"? I asked. "Just write it on the receipt copy", he said. "And if I split a tip let's say to the waiter, the receptionist, and the cook, I just write it down and each will get their tip", I asked. "Yes sir that is all you do", he replied. I wrote down a five credit tip for Peter, three for the cook and two credits for the receptionist. Peter said, "thank you Mark". "Have a great day", I said while walking out the door.

When I got back to the research area Sunshine was working like an ant. She had already put most of the generator together. We talked about the generator and what the alloy could be used for while we ate. After we ate, I said", Sunshine, would you get that cart over there and something rubber to lay the generator on. Do not hook the battery until I get back and check the magnets, okay. I need to get over to the science lab and check on my other project." "Okay boss", she said.

When I got over to the lab, Judy was working on the spectrometer and going back and forth to the microscope. "Hey Mark, glad you are here. You will be excited to see this specimen under the microscope. This is a slice of the meat from yesterday. I guess because it set out overnight, the algae or whatever it is, is growing rapidly. Look at the specimen you placed in the dark at 98.6 degrees. It actually started growing around the edges and is starting to change color. I think we have a winner. Jeff over there is a genius and he has never seen anything like it. By the way, your nurse, girlfriend got me the blood that we needed quickly", she said with a sheepish grin. "How does the blood look", I said. It all has the same familiarities except those samples from the west side of the city. The adult smear from the east side is less in quantity of the unidentified composition than the child so far not diagnosed. I am attempting to break down the composition and then we can make sure. I got a sample of the dome material to test as well. All in all, I think we found the cause", she said. We just must find a cure", I said.

"You know that generator that you said was impossible. It is just about ready for a demonstration. I will call you when it is ready", I said. "I would love to see it. I promise not to laugh if it flubs out", Judy said with a bright smile. I went back to the technology area and helped Sunshine finish the model. She did most of the work. It just seems harder than what it looks. We turned on the machine and it hummed and vibrated. I calibrated the magnets until all you heard was a light hum. With the casing, you will probably not know it was there. I pick up the phone and called Judy. She came right over. "You have got to be kidding me Mark. That thing can't provide the electricity you were talking about", Judy said. "Then you are really going to be surprised", Sunshine said. I just smiled and headed over to Jodi. "Jodi, I need to do a test and I will need all the electric power in the room", I said. She said it was okay to let the others know before I did anything. "Listen up everyone. I need to do a power test. It will only take a few minutes. Would you please stop what you doing if it is electrical or finish up quickly if you are in the middle of something important, I said. All but one person finished. A few moments later, he said he was done. Sunshine had already taken the generator over by the breaker box. "Okay Sunshine, cut the breaker", I said. She cut the breaker and it went dark. She then hooked up the cables to the breaker box. "Ready", she said. "Okay, cross your fingers and start it up", I said. She pressed the start button. The rod went up and down faster and faster until there was just a hum. She flipped the switch and the lights came on getting brighter and brighter. Everyone in the room was laughing, smiling, talking and some clapped yelling yeah. "Okay, put the breaker back on", I said. The lights were still bright with no change. "Judy, would you check the unit next door please", I said. She came back saying that everyone was wondering why the lighting was so bright. "I don't know how far this machine is affecting the light, but we know it works. Ladies and gentlemen, this is the first perpetual generator ever made", I said. You could not hear yourself think with all the noise going on all around with everyone cheering, talking, yelling and laughing. Judy came up and gave me a great big hug, kisses and congratulations. Sunshine came over and shook my hand. "No way Sunshine, I need a big hug and a kiss," I said. Sunshine smiled and gave me a big hug and a warm kiss.

I went to the phone and called the Governor's office. "Hi Carol, "is the Governor back yet", I said. "Yes, he came in about an hour ago. He wants to see you right away", she said. I told her I would be right over and thanked Judy, Sunshine and Jodi and said I would see everyone later. I went right over to the tower. "Go right in", Carol said as I entered in the executive area. I tapped on the door and walked in. "Have a good trip Governor", I said. "Corporate wants you to go to Antonio right away", he said. "What's up", I said. I told the President what you did for my daughter. He told me that his 21 year old daughter had that lung disease and another two children had died from it. He wants you to heal his daughter. He is scared", the Governor said. "I need you to stop for a moment and take a deep breath. Is his daughter critical? If not, do you think you can hold him off until next week?" I said. "I don't think she is critical, but I will call him", he said.

"Would you ask Mr. Wright and Carol to come in if possible? I have a lot of things to tell you that have happen over the last two days", I said. He picked up the phone and called Carol and she called Mr. Wright. They both came in at the same time. "I want to thank you again Mr. Wright for helping me get started the other day", I said. "No problem, I am glad I could help", he said. "I am pretty certain that we have found out what is causing the lung disease. If so, we should be able to come up with a cure soon", I said. Everyone congratulated me. While they were still talking, I interrupted. "I have two more announcements to make. I have created a perpetual generator that will solve a ton of problems in the city and a new alloy that can be used in many ways. Both should save and make a great deal of money for the corporation. If I do not have to go to corporate tomorrow, I would like to have a demonstration and make the announcements to the Directors tomorrow at 11 AM if possible", I said. "I knew there was something about you Mark", the Governor said with a smile, "but I could not put my finger on it. I will delay the trip to Antonio and you will have your day", he said. "Besides the Directors, I would like to invite Judy Mimms, Mandy Collins, and Heddi Scott, who we call Sunshine. Those ladies were instrumental in my projects. "No problem", the Governor said. "This city might have to proclaim a Mark Anglin day", Mrs. Wright, laughed.

"I am so excited. Let's all have lunch after the meeting", the Governor said. "Are we actually going to have lights", Carol said. "All the light you want Carol", I said. We all went over to the executive dining hall. I ordered catfish for everyone. Judy was not sure if she liked fish or not. After first bite, she had a new favorite. After lunch, I gave the Governor and LT Governor a hug when they reached to shake hands, this caught them off guard. I gave Carol a warm hug and said I would see them tomorrow. I told Sunshine on the way back to technology she could take the rest of the day off if she wanted to that she did a fantastic job. I told her I needed her to wear something nicer tomorrow or bring a change of clothes for the demonstration and lunch. When we got back to technology, we put the generator in a secure room. Sunshine gave me another hug and said goodbye. "Well Judy, I guess we had a small day of fame. I guess it is time we get back to work", I said. On the way out I gave a lady I did not know and Jodi a hug and Judy and I treaded off to the science lab. We went over and over the findings we had and still could not figure out how that whatever it is worked. It grew fast like a virus and algae should not be able to live in heavy chlorine. It was about 7 PM when a lady working at the station next to me started slapping things around. "I just can't figure it out. It should be easy, but I just can't see it" she said. "Would you mind", I ask as she moved away and allowed me to see what she was doing. She was looking at a seed, trying to figure out why it was not germinating. I noticed the seed coat and the radicle were already turning brown. "The seeds are already bad. You need new seeds", I said. "How are you trying to germinate them", I said. "Under a bright light", she said. Plants need photosynthesis. Ultraviolet light outside puts off different colors that may not be observant from the naked eye, but range from red to dark blue, so take a light fixture and die the shield lets say a light to dark blue, not the bulb. Painting the bulb would cause gas and finally burn off", I said. She said thank you and went into the storeroom and came out with what looked like a bathroom light fixture. She took a blue magic marker and painted the fixture. I guess that will work I thought. She put a bulb in the fixture and turned on the light. "How long do I need to wait", she said. "It will take two to 3 days and you should start seeing some germination', I said.

As Judy and I were finishing up, she said, "let's get a drink." "Okay", I said as we were walking to the door. Once outside I headed for the club. "Where are you going", she said. "To the club", I said. "The only club over there is the executive club. Are you an executive", she said. "I don't know what I am, I just seem to go where I please and no one really questions me. I guess, I always look like I know what I am doing. Maybe because I really don't care", I smiled. She did not question me anymore. We got to the club and found a table close to the bar. The waitress asked me for my card. I gave her the card and she came back in a few moments and handed it back and ask what we would like to drink. Judy ordered bourbon and seven and I ordered a light beer. As we are sitting there, the band seemed to be warming up. After a while, I figured out that they were just practicing. I guess the band plays maybe only on weekends. We set there for a while talking and my mind kept going back to the band. My other self-starting thinking at the same time it seemed. The music in this place really needs help, I thought. I had another personality pop up in my head. Back in high school and at the university, I was in a six band and I was the lead singer. Later I became an entertainer. I wonder if I could still sing I thought. I used to play the piano, guitar and the trumpet. Judy was talking about where she was from and her family. When she started talking about ex-boyfriends, my mind drifted again. "I want to go over and talk to the band," I said as I was getting up. Judy grabbed my hand and we walked over to where some of the band was practicing. There was a song in my mind I used to sing all the time and loved, "My Heart Goes On and On." I ask a gray hair gentleman if I could use his piano for a moment. First he scooted over, then stood up as I sat down and moved in behind me. Judy leaned over the piano by my side. It felt like the old days, now if I can sing I was reassuring myself. When I started singing, one of the band members moved a microphone in front of me. Judy said that was beautiful. When I got done with the song, people stood up and applauded me. One of the musicians asked me to play another. I sang "Close Yet So Far" and "Kiss Me Goodbye." These were songs not sang in this world. I guess I got into my own singing. When I looked up, people were standing all around me smiling and clapping. I then notice the LT Governor with I guessed his wife. As we were walking away, you could hear people making sounds like awe and some asking for more. I said, "I do not want to spoil everyone and I shall return. Thank you all very much. "I went over to him with Judy tailing me and he put out his hand to shake, but I hugged him. "Who is this beautiful young lady", I teased. "This is Marilyn my wife," he said. "It is a pleasure. This is Judy and you have already met Mr. Wright", I said. "Call me Jerry," he said. "Come and sit with us for a bit", he said.

"What is it that you don't do Mark?" Jerry asked. "I do not play the violin sir", I replied. I guess it was funny because they laughed at it. An old joke I thought. "You sing beautifully", Marilyn said. "Thank you", I said. While I got your attention Mark, I need to ask you a real big personal favor", he said. "I will do anything within reason Jerry", I said. "You helped Milea, can you see if you can help Marilyn", he said. "Now Jerry", she said. I asked Marilyn to stand up. "In a moment I want you to hug me like you hug Jerry, your mom, dad or someone you love, and really mean it. I want you then to take a deep breath in as much as possible through the nose and breathe out very slowly through your mouth and release me very, slowly. Will you do that?" I asked. Marilyn came close and hugged. I could feel her energy. She took a deep breath and we slowly stepped away from each other. I fell to the floor. Jerry and Judy helped me up to a chair. I nearly blacked out. I don't remember doing that before. "I am so sorry Marilyn. How long did they give you?" I asked probably looking drunk right now. "One beer was just too much" I sort of squeezed out my tight lips like I was hit in the stomach. "The doctor told me about three weeks or so a week ago", she said with tears in her eyes. I sat there for a moment. My brain seemed to explode with thousands of thoughts all at one time. I held my head and stooped over. "Are you okay?" Judy asked.

I grabbed Marilyn's hands and set her in the chair next to me. "I need you to understand something. You are very, very important to me. All lives are important to me. I am working on some projects right now that could save thousands of people's lives. Whenever I attempt a healing such as yours, I am sick and in pain for hours or days. It will finally go away like a virus, but I am still sick. With that being said, I could not attempt a full healing until maybe after Wednesday next week if I do not have to go to corporate. What I will do for you is give you a little treatment each day until I can get the whole healing, if that is okay Marilyn", I said with glassy eyes. "Mark, I do not want anyone to suffer from my problems", she said. "Let's go to your residence and let me work on you for a moment, would that be okay Judy?" I said. "Do you want me to come", she asked. "If they say it is okay", I replied. "Sure, you may come Judy", Marilyn said.

When we got to the residence, I could tell Marilyn was in a great deal of pain. I sat her down and Jerry got her some water and a pain pill. "I don't know what Jerry told you about me or what he really knows, but what I am going to tell you is going to be very unorthodox. Your brain actually does the healing. We will be using my energy to I guess you can say to speak to yours and tell it what to do. Healing cancer is one of the worst for me. It takes a great deal of energy and it causes me a great deal of pain. That is why I can't help you heal all at once. When I start doing major healing on you, your cells and nerves come back alive and you may feel a great deal of pain associated with that, but it will only last a few hours at a time. You could possibly bleed or have some kind of mucus come out of your mouth, ears, eyes, and private parts; any place you an opening. If a doctor where to check he would not find a break anywhere from where the fluids come from. That is the bad draining from your body. It does not happen to everyone, but it happens. Also, I cannot help everyone for some reason, I don't know why. When we start off, you will need to strip from the neck to your waist. I will be bare chested also. We will hug each other for long periods of time. When I ask you about energy, please be very truthful. When I ask if you feel the energy, you say yes or no. When I ask you how much energy you feel coming into you or leaving you, try to give me some estimate in your own words. If I ask you what your pain level is from one to ten, please try to be realistic. Do you understand'? I said. "Yes", she said. Do you want to go in another room or do you want to do it here?" I asked. "Here is okay", she said. She shifted her wig to make it look nice then took off her blouse and bra. She had a beautiful body even after losing a lot of weight. What a time to be healing, I thought.

After hugging for about fifteen minutes, I used my hands to move the energy from her body. I did that until I had tears coming from my eyes. I had to quit. "Do you have a wheel chair?" I asked. "What is a wheel chair", Jerry asked. You would think they would have invented a wheel chair, I thought. "No matter Jerry, I will get someone to make you one", I said. "Marilyn, I need you to go to the hospital daily and get a tech to scan your cancers. Get me a copy of pictures if you can", I said. I sat there for a moment holding my upper stomach. I had a headache from hell. Jerry and Marilyn both thanked me and Judy and I were out the door. "Let me help you to your cubicle", Judy said. "House, apartment, residence, please call it anything but cubicle", I said. I said I could make it, but she went with me anyway. I went into the bedroom and fell on the bed. About 2 in the morning I awoke with someone nudging up against me. I glanced to the side and Judy was snuggled up to my chest. We still had our clothes on. I was totally tired and fell back to sleep.

CHAPTER 7   Things Were About To Change

The alarm went off at 6 AM and both Judy and I jumped up at the same time. We looked at each other for just a moment, and then Judy asked, "are you okay Mark." "Yes Judy, thank you, do you want the shower first." No, I will get one back at my place. I just stayed to make sure you were alright", she said, kissed me on the cheek and was out the door. I showered and put on a suit. I thought I would put my coveralls on when I get to work and I would be ready for the meeting at 11 AM. I got to the tech area about 8 AM. Jodi gave me a hug coming in the door. She said good morning and I headed back to my cubby hole. Sunshine heard me coming and stood up from what she was doing and gave me a hug. I think I have most the ladies trained I thought. "What would you like me to do boss?" she said. "I need to use that beautiful brain of yours Sunshine", I said. I went to the drafting table and drew out a picture as close as I could of a wheelchair. "Do you think we could find some individuals to build this thing yesterday?" I said. "You getting lazy in your young age boss?" she said. "The chair is for someone sick and in pain, so they can get back and forth to the hospital", I said. She said, "that is a good idea. They should make lots of these. If I can't do it, I will find someone that can", she said. "It does not have to be perfect, but I sure could use one yesterday", I asked. "Try to get some people to brainstorm it and you need to get back here and bring the generator to the meeting by 11 AM", I said. "You got it boss", she said as she nearly ran out the door. I went to the draft board and drew specs for an anti-gravity car. It did not need to be perfect, but enough to show people what it looked like.

10 AM came quickly. I went ahead over to the tower. When I got there, it seemed in turmoil. I saw six directors, and a dozen or so managers. I did not invite the managers, I thought. There were four men and one lady in suits by Carol's desk. As I walked up, two other men in suits came out of the office with the Governor. "There he is", the Governor said. "Mark, this is Mr. Preston, President and Mr. Kilby, one of the vice-presidents of the Corporation." Walking out, he introduced me to the executives standing by Carol's Desk. "They will be sitting in on your little meeting today Mark", he said. They headed for the conference room. "Hold, I would like to start the meeting from here if you do not mind", I asked. Judy, Mrs. Wright's secretary went into the conference room and brought out the directors in there. Judy and Sunshine came in the door with the generator. "Ladies and Gentlemen, this is Judy Mimms and Heddi Scott who we call Sunshine they are my associates who helped make the meeting happen", I said. "Wow Sunshine, you look great", I whispered. I turned around and made an announcement. "The lights are going to go out for a few minutes. If you are working on anything electrical, please stop what you are doing or quickly finish up. Sunshine and Judy pushed the model of the generator over to the breaker box. "Everyone ready", Judy said. Judy pulled the breaker and Sunshine attached the cables to the breaker box. Sunshine pressed the starter button and the engine hummed and the lights got brighter and brighter, brighter than they have ever been. "This generator was started from a nine volt battery. This is just a model without the shell. It is a perpetual electromagnet and regular magnets", I said. "You will notice, it has only a few moving parts; the two fans and the rod. These are the only items that must probably be replaced after years of service. The manufactured model could be as small or smaller than the model up to as large as you need it to be", I said. "Now Sunshine and Janet, would you turn on the breaker", I said.

Janet flipped the breaker and there was no change in the power. "Would someone call a few floors down and ask them how their lights are", I asked. Two ladies said the lights were brighter there also. "I don't know how many floors are affected by the generator, but I bet they are really happy right now", I commented. "I am impressed", said the President. "As a matter of fact, I am more than impressed", he said. "We can now go to the conference room, ladies, make sure no one touches that generator or they could get a terrible bite", I said as I was waving the President and other executives through the door. All the directors, six corporate people, secretaries, Judy, Sunshine and myself. That made for a full room, but we all fitted at the large conference table. Mandy showed up in the nick of time for the meeting.

I came here this morning because of a call from Ralph stating that Mark Anglin would not come to Antonio, that he had found the cause of the sickness. We have had many people dying from that disease and many, many more sick including my daughter right now. Then I get here and Mr. Anglin has yet another surprise for me", he said. "Mr. Anglin, you have my attention. Before anyone else talks, I want to hear a briefing from Mark Anglin", he said.

"First of all Mandy Collins, nurse and Judy Mimms, scientist where the two people that helped with finding the cause of the disease, I could have not done it alone. I realize it only took two days, but through many hours of slaving we accomplished our task", I said. "Hell, we had hundreds of people working night and day for months trying to find the cure and they could not even figure out what it was. Ralf has a great staff here", the President delightfully said. "We still have not found a cure, but we have at least a few good ideas. At least we know how to stop the disease from continuing", I said. The areas in the different cities that have generators being cooled by the reservoirs are the problem. I believe Antonio City has two which probably is why you have more sickness. These areas must be completely sealed off from the city. Now after they are sealed off, the city must probably have humidifiers or some misters to keep the humidity at least fifteen percent. Otherwise people will get dry coughs and we will have another problem. I believe Doctor Williams and Doctor Roberts will testify to that", I said. They both shook their heads. If you are not aware of this; there are probably thousands of people infected with the disease we are not aware. It has not gotten bad enough to have them checked yet. Look around at all the people coughing in the city", I said. "Also ladies and gentlemen, the dome or bubble around the city could be causing health problems. First, it is a matter of fresh air and the second is ultra violet light. Now that we have electricity, it would be a good idea to have lights with a blue hue around the city. The blue color will give us the highest color on the chart of light from the sun hitting the planet, which plants need to grow and certain parts of our bodies need to be healthy. We are not sure about the makeup of the dome, if it causes health problems. We just know the combination of the chlorine from the reservoirs causes problems", I said.

"Before I or my associates answer any questions, let me give you a short brief on the generators. Heddi Scott, who we call Sunshine because when Sunshine comes into a place everything lights up. Sunshine was there every minute working to complete that project. She was working off of my drafts when I wasn't there working on the disease completing and even using her ingenuity to advance the project. I do not know how much energy the generators will produce. Utilities can figure that out so we know how many to produce. The city has only one grid. If something major were to happen to the electricity, the whole city must shut down. Separating the city into different grids would help prevent any catastrophes. Portable units can be made to just plug in where needed and you have instant light. This should save the corporation millions and possibly make them millions over the years", I said. We also came up with a new alloy. This new alloy could be as thin as a piece of paper and be as strong as five inches of steel. This is what we will make the casing for the generators. It could be used to build airplanes, automobiles and more. It could also make the corporation millions", I said.

"Now I will take questions until lunch if you like", I said. I answered many questions until lunch, most the same, but presented differently. When we broke for lunch, some seemed disappointed that their questions were not answered. I just told them to submit me questions or wait until we have another meeting. The president asked me to meet someone before lunch, so we went to the Governor's office. He introduced me to his wife and daughter. His wife was about five foot ten, beautiful, great body and about forty years old. His daughter was twenty one and a carbon copy of his wife. I hugged his wife, then his daughter. I asked his daughter though to take a deep breath and breathe out slowly as she released. "When is the last time you saw a doctor?" I asked. "It's been about a month. Doctor just said it would get worst", she said. "I want you to hug me again, this time longer, and then slowly release as you are breathing out", I said. This time I had to sit down and rub the energy from my arms. "Mr. Preston, I recommend she see the doctor today please. I need to confirm something", I said. "What is wrong?" he said. I walked him to the side of the office. "I think she also has cancer just below the lungs", I said. His eyes got big and glassy. "If you can help my daughter Mark, I will give you anything you want. My family is more important than the corporation", he said. I thought he would cry. Have Carol make an appointment for her after lunch", I said to the Governor.

Make sure you tell them it is for the President's daughter. Please also ask that we have an additional appointment around 3 PM and have Dr. Roberts and possibly Dr. Williams available. "Let's try to calm down and get through lunch. I will be over at the hospital at 3 PM I said. I want you to know Mr. Preston, I will do whatever I can for your daughter Sandra", I said. "I will give you whatever you want Mark", he whispered to me as I was leaving. Lunch ran over with all the questions. Mr. Preston was very quiet. As I was about to leave, the Governor ask me to come to his office. We first spoke briefly about the President's daughter. Then I mention I was also working with Marilyn and that it would take a toll on me. I reminded him I absorb a lot of pain and discomfort when I am doing these healings. I might not be able to think and do my job properly for a few days. "Mark, I need to tell you something else. The president has authorized me to give you some bonuses for your excellent work. You will receive 150,000 a month for a year for the disease and 100,000 for the generator. You will probably get a bonus for the alloy as well. You will be making more than me", he said with a smile. Could I have 25,000 paid to Judy and Mandy for helping me the disease and 25,000 to Sunshine for helping with the generator", I said. "You do not have to pay them anything. They are regular employees", he said. "I want them to have the money. Would you please make it happen", I said. "It will start not this Friday, but next payday Friday, okay?" he said. "I have one more favor sir. I need to see if I can get a room or building to work out of that is at least three thousand square feet or more. I need it secured. I would like to have Judy and Sunshine assigned to work with me permanently for now if possible?" I asked. I then left the office and headed for the tech area. Sunshine was fiddling with something as I entered. "Hey boss", she said. "Sunshine, would you please start getting some materials together for me. This is the draft of the anti-gravity car. Here is a grocery list of materials I believe I will need. Please let no one know what you are doing. Just tell people you are keeping busy until I get back. I need to be gone for a few days. I might check in, but I am not sure. The suits have me doing them a favor. If you need me or need anything, please call Carol or Judy at the tower and they will help you the best they can. Sunshine, thank you again for all you do", I said as I was hugging her goodbye.

I got to the hospital just before 3 PM. Everyone was already there. Sandra was in a hospital gown. "Hi everyone", I said as I entered. What I will do today may only be a part of the healing. We may have to do this again tomorrow or even for a few days or more. The side effects for Sandra could be bad pain and discomforts for a few hours. She may also bleed or have mucus come from face and private areas. Some people do, some don't, I think it has to do with the type of energy a person has. I will first pinch Sandra's back just below the brain stem, then I will hold her in an embrace bare-chested until I fill the energy exchanging between us. The simplest way to explain it is, my body and mind sends her body and mind messages in the way of energy telling her how to heal herself. I know it sounds weird, but it works. I had doctors tell me there is no way it will work. I ask you doctors here to show you how it works", I said.

I had Sandra move her gown down to her waist and I removed my shirt. What I need you to do Sandra is hug me like your hugging someone you love. When I ask, take a deep, deep breath in through your nose and hold it and then breathe out slowly through your mouth. At the same time release me very, slowly, okay?" I ask. "I understand", she said. I moved close to her and we embraced. She shook I guess in fear. It took about fifteen minutes before I could feel the energy exchanging in our bodies. I could feel her pain. I held it as long as I could and ask her to take a deep breath. We released slowly and as we broke free, I fell to the floor. I hate working with cancer, I thought. They could see the tears coming from my eyes and ask if I was okay. They helped me up to a chair. I ask the doctor for a few pain pills. "How do you feel Sandra", I asked. "Actually I feel really, really good. I do not feel any pain at all. I feel like I have a swelling right here", she said touching the area above the stomach. "Doc, would you please scan her and see what the change is", I asked. Doc had a tech come in and scanned her. The diseased area was completely gone, but the cancer was still there. "You can see the receding of the cancer", Doc said. "Unbelievable, I would not have believed it if I did not see it for myself. Makes you feel like you did not pay attention in class", Doctor Williams said. "I will not be able to do anymore today for Sandra. "If I try to do too much, it could make me very sick or kill me and I need to give Sandra a day to move the energy around and then we will do it again. Mr. Preston's wife started crying. Mr. Preston went over to her and held her. Sandra also hugged both of them. "We will never forget this", Mr. Preston said. "I need to go lie down and rest", I said as I was walking out the door. Doctor Williams followed me out the door. "If you need anything Mark, please give me a call", she said. I thanked her and headed home. I guess I made another friend, I thought.

I laid down for two hours and headed to Mr. Wright's apartment. "Hi Mark", Marilyn said as she opened the door. "Come on in. Jerry and Ralph are meeting with the President right now. Can I get you anything", she asked. "I came over to do a healing with you", I said. "I have been so excited about the healing, especially after hearing about Sandra. What do you want me to do?" she asked. "You need to be bare from the neck to the waist. It will only take about fifteen minutes", I said. She took all her clothes off and stood there with her panties swinging around on her pointer finger. I tried to keep my mind on the healing. "I need you to hug me hard until I tell you to take a deep breath and breathe out slowly and at the same time release slowly", I ask. I took off my shirt and she wrapped her arms around me. She put her mouth up to my neck which made me uneasy. "Please turn your head outward", I asked. She held me tight. About ten or fifteen minutes passed and I could feel the energy exchanging, then the pain set in. I held as long as possible, then told her to take a deep breath. As she was releasing, tears came from my eyes and everything went dark. I don't know how long I was out, but I awoke with Marilyn running her fingers through my hair. Marilyn's foot was by my head and as my eyes cleared. I had pubic hair nearly staring me in the face. "You know if you shaved off that bush, Jerry might pay attention to you more", I said sort of nervously. "I will let you show me sometime", she teased. I got up and sat in a chair. Marilyn put her clothes back on, moving as to make sure I was watching every move. "Are you okay", she asked as I slowly stood up. "I need to go back home and rest a while", I said. "Okay Mark. Thank you again. I will let Jerry know you came by," she said as I opened the door and headed out. When I got home, Mandy was sitting at the table and stood up. "I have been waiting for you. I missed you", she said. "I am sorry I have not been paying much attention to you. I just came from Mrs. Wright. I was working on her cancer. I am exhausted", I said. "We can talk later. Come in here and lay down", she ushered me. I was out like a light. I woke up about 2 AM and Mandy was lying beside me. When I moved, she opened her eyes. "Where is Tabitha", I asked. "I left her at the Children's Center. I wanted to spend some time with you", she said. Mandy came up over my chest and started lightly kissing me. "What about little Carol", I asked. "Melissa will drop her off at the Children's Center", she said as she kissed me even more passionate. "You just lay back and relax", she said. She moved up on top of me. We made love and fell asleep in each other's arms. The alarm went off at 6 AM.

I turned off the alarm and laid back down. "Don't get up", she said. I felt her warm mouth come over me and we made love again. I heard the phone ringing and I got up. "We will be having a meeting at 9 AM. I was not able to contact Mandy. If you can contact her, the President wants all from yesterday's meeting available this morning", Carol said. "I will be there and will try to contact Mandy", I said. I woke Mandy and told her about the meeting.

CHAPTER 8   A New Era

Except for Mandy, I think I am the last to get to the conference room. "Let's settle down", the Governor said. Mandy just walked in. Everyone was still shuffling around nervously. The President entered and sat down. "It seems we have some unfinished business and we need to weight out some grievances by some of our Directors", he said. "We will just go around the room starting with Ryan. Mark will go last. I need to know what unfinished business we have and anything else that is on your mind. Judy whispered in my ear that the tissue samples in the lab had died. She thought it was from the blue light from the seed experiment. "I don't have anything else Governor. Mark's announcement already put a feather in my cap", he said. "Kelly", the Governor said. "As you know Governor, manufacturing is already loaded down. We are told to stop most everything we are doing to get this new generator that Anglin came up with a priority. Mr. Anglin seems to think that we work for him. I think we need to look at what is a real priority here and who is in charge", he said. "Dr. Williams, what have you got", the Governor said. "As for Mark Anglin, I did not trust him at first meeting and would not have given him the time of day. He has proven himself an asset to the city not only with his new generator, but help solving the disease we have been working on for nearly five years. I would like to also say, we need to do something about staff. We cannot expect our doctors and nurses to keep working like they have been. Thank you, Governor", she said. "Big John, I heard you have complaints", he said. "While we are discussing Mr. Anglin, I have not liked him since he came here. He has been here a week and has already effecting how this city is run. We ran it fine before he came along. Now we have to shore up that generator pond and that will slow construction. We have enough personnel to get the jobs we are currently working on. That is all", he said. "Billy, what have you got to say? You have some questions", the Governor said. "I will first say this. "As for Mark Anglin, I don't know him. I have seen him and said hi. That is all, but everyone I talk to seems to like him. He is just one of those likeable people. What I would like to bring up though is we are having some real employee problems. As you know, the Bulkhead section of the city was out of electricity for two days. I have nearly a riot on my hands and could lose thousands of employees if we do not do something fast. We are already shorthanded as it is. I need help in this matter", he said.

"Mr. Cooley", the Governor said. "Well, we are shorthanded also, but the committee voted to hold employee numbers at a percentage to save money. I like Mr. Anglin's new generator. I know though, it is going to take a while to get them built and in place. In the meantime, we need help sir", he said. "Betty, do you have anything to add", the Governor said. "Other than the point I have been making for a while now, is that we need to step up recruiting new students for the University. Thank you", she said. "Sharon", the Governor said. "I know a lot of you have a problem with your employee percentages, but we have to stay in budget. As for the unrest in service, you are going to have to get a handle on it Mr. Woods", she said. "Mr. Anglin, you said you would like to say a few words", the Governor said.

"Well, after listening to the directors, I may have more than a few words. First of all I am sorry some of you don't like me. When I came here, I did it to help this city, to help the people within it. I did not come here for glory, fame, I wasn't looking for the Governor's job nor was it for money. I have already turned down more money the first day than I than I had made in nearly two years. My granddad used to say that you treat people nice and most will come back and treat you nice. You just have to hope that the few you couldn't win may finally come around. He also said that if I see something wrong, that I should stand up and make myself heard and be firm about it. Well, my granddad was never wrong in anything that he said that I know of, so here it goes. Everyone seems to have a manpower problem. From what I hear, you caused that problem by voting to cut manpower and save money. Let me ask you all a question. If I could show you a way to save this city a billion credits a year, would you listen to me? Would that make your day", I said. "If you could show us that, I would vote for it", John Ryan said. A few directors shook their heads. I did not tell you where the savings were coming from", I said. "Let me ask you this. What do you think President Preston and the stockholders of this corporation would say if they say a billion credit savings on the profit and loss statement?" I said. "We could all possibly get a raise", Sharon said. What do you think would stick out the most on the P&L statement folks?" I said. "The savings", Ryan said "Let me tell you something ladies and gentlemen, the president, his managing partners and the board of directors care a rats ass about a billion dollar savings. What they look at first is the bottom line, profit and loss. If there is no profit, the rest of the P&L is worthless. If this corporation is not making a profit, the board of directors are looking for a new president and managing partners. The savings I was talking about is to cut all employees from the city. No employees, no cost and plenty of savings, but no one to make any profit. I will probably get fired for the next statement, but it has to be said. You as a board are responsible for aiding the Governor to make the right decisions about employees have failed. The Governor and LT Governor failed when they did not research the cuts, the president failed when they put a budget on the city. First of all, all cities are different. Each city should have a budget on the percentage of production, size and population", I said. Bill said, "can I get a word in?" "Not yet, I want to finish while I am on a roll. Let me start with Billy Woods and services. How would every one of you here like to spend two days in the Bulkhead with no electricity? Twenty thousand or more souls in that section of the city without electricity, unable to cook, no refrigeration, no water and no sewer is unthinkable. I would not live there. I would quit and go back to where I came from. Services need at least four Directors instead of one for 60,000 employees, that's crazy. As for helping services Mr. Woods, I would be happy to speak to your workers. Most of those people came from the outside. They either owned or worked for businesses shut down because of the Corporation coming in with products and services cheaper than they could furnish them for and ended up working for the Man. They were already unhappy when they got here. My family has a business they have been running for three generations. Profit from that business now barely supports the family. I know those people and I believe I can help to get them to come to at least and halfway bargaining point where all can walk away happy if the committee trust me and would support my decisions. Talk about profit. If you think services make no profit other than food services. You are wrong if you think that. What does it cost to retain new employees, especially if you are retaining 20% or more a month? You need the place clean to attract the outsiders coming into the city to shop. Other than taxes and rent, where do you think the majority of the profits come from people? They come from people spending money in the shops around the city. It really looks good when they come to the city and there are no lights and the shops are closed. They don't keep walking two or three miles down the boardwalk to find a shop. They go back home. While I am on that, I believe the first ten or more generators out of manufacturing should go to the Bulkhead. The losses in that area must be astronomical. This city should also have at least six entrances instead of two, to get more people in and make it easier for people to shop. More people shopping more profit for the city. Also, if there were to be an emergency like that in Paso city, there would be no way that over two million people could get out in time. I could build you buses so customers coming to the city can get around quicker and carrying products easier. More employees in construction will help profits by getting more people to live here. More people more credits. We need more employees to make more profit. That is the bottom line", I said.

One more item before you fire me. I believe we need to hire recruiters to go out to the high schools with some type of evaluation those students can take. Please do not call it a test. You will scare them off. Find out somewhat what a student's IQ is, and possibly what sector they might be good to work in. Offer a bonus at the end of first year to the students who come to work. For those with a good IQ, offer free college. For each year they get free college, they sign a contract to work for the corporation for two or two and half years. Also while those students are in school, they need a place to live, food and entertainment. Have them working in the different divisions to pay for their room and board. A lot of students won't even try in high school, because they know that they cannot afford college. Why study if they are going to work a minimal job anyways. This is a great chance to get them started. You may say, country hicks becoming doctors, scientist and engineers. I have only a high school education. I am able to build generators, create new alloys and work in a lab to find a cure for diseases without any additional school. Everything I know, I learned from books in the library or from listening to other people. You can't judge a person by where they come from. Besides you never know what that old country hick or even a child may know. My granddad had been working on a generator for over ten years. One day he was in the barn cussing, because he just could not figure it out. I was sitting there watching him and pulled out a round magnet I have in my pocket and told him to try this. It will pull that pole down. I was six years old. A light went off in his head and he took the magnets and other magnets and completed the generator I made for you, except mine looked a lot better. My granddad died two years later and when I was fourteen, the generator quit working. I found out why it quit working and built a new one and it is still working today, nearly ten years later. I am sorry for the story to prove a point. How many of you know that we have nurses, that would love to go to school to be doctors, and people with a great mechanical or building background wanted to go to college to be engineers or even just better themselves. We have no doctor or nursing school in the city and that must change. That will give the hospital a lot more staff and part-time nurses while those students are going to school. It is great training also. You all need to stop complaining and sit down with the Governor, LT Governor and the President and his managing staff and work out your problems now before it is too late. My grandpa always said that two heads are better than one and people working together like family could solve the problems of the world. Bottom line ladies and gentlemen, dad leaves for work in the morning and tells wife he is excited to get on those floors and make them shine. Lady tells husband, I am going to cook a meal that will thrill the taste buds of every person in the dining hall and the director comes home and says honey, I had a great day. I accomplished everything I started out to do and I helped a thousand people all at the same time. I am sure I left a lot of things out, but I am sure they will come to me", I said with a smile and sat down.

Carol then whispered something to the president and she came to Mandy and I. We were asked to come outside. The president told everyone to take a 15 minute break. When I went out front, Mrs. Preston and Sandra were there. I had forgotten about helping her this morning. Carol went back out and asked Dr. Williams and Roberts to come. I told them I could do it from one of the offices. We went back to the spare office that the president was using. Sandra and I both got bare-chested. We hugged for a moment and then pulled away. "The cancer is actually smaller now than last I felt it yesterday", I said. We hugged this time hard exchanging energy. When Sandra released, it felt like the cancer just popping out of her. I had felt nothing like it. At least it was not as painful as yesterday. I sat in the chair for a few moments. "Judy was telling me that the tissue samples that we had with the growth on it died. We think it was from the blue glass. That is probably why I had an easier time pulling the growth from Sandra. When you all left Antonio, you were in the sun light off and on. The sun kills the growth", I said. "Let Mandy go back with you to the hospital and get your stomach scanned." They left with Mandy and were saying thank you as they walked out the door.

"Worried about going back in there Mark", Mr. Preston said. "No sir, I can handle it", I said. Mr. Preston smiled at me and patted me on the back as we walked into the conference room. Everyone was back except Mandy who went to the hospital. John Cooley started to talked. "Let's hold everything ladies and gentlemen. It's close to lunch, we will continue at 1 PM", the president said. At lunch, Mr. Preston asked me to sit with him, the Governor, Lt Governor, Marilyn, Marque, and Sandra. I was wondering what everyone was going to say about this, I thought. When Sandra came up, she was jumping up and down like a school girl. She came over, held my cheeks and kissed me on the lips telling me it was gone over and over. Marque looked like she had been crying. "Thank you so much, Mark. You will always be special in our hearts", she said.

Peter, the waiter came up and gave me a hug and asked what we would like to drink. He said he would be right back for our order. Big Mike came out of the kitchen loud as usual. "Mark, I have a special lunch for you. I make the very best country steak in Texans", He said. He nearly pulled me out of the chair to hug me in a bear hug. He is the size of a bear, I thought. "I hope you saved Doc a steak?" I asked. "I always have country steak for Doc", he said. "Mike, this is the President, his wife and daughter and of course you know the Governor, LT Governor, and his wife. Mike is the head chef for this dining facility", I said. "Are you the head guy for this city?" Mike asked. "Yes I am", the President smiled. "I will give you the second biggest steak", he said. "Who gets the biggest steak", the President asked. "Mark, of course. You have a beautiful wife and daughter. Children are so important Mr. President", said Mike. "Would all of you like to try my steak? It is the best country steak in Texans", he said. "We will all try your steak", said the Governor. Mike left and headed back to the kitchen with a big smile on his face. "He has eleven children. He loves kids. He works six to seven days a week to make sure they are taken care", I said. "Everyone here seems to love you", said the President. "I always take the time to tell each one of them how great a job they are doing; I shake their hands or give them a hug whenever I see them. It sure puts everyone in a good mood. That is what I was trying to tell them in the meeting. Treat people nice and they will in most cases treat you nice", I said.

About fifteen minutes past and Peter came out with a cart. Eyes widened when the plates were put on the table. Chicken fried stakes are large anyway. There were also, mashed potatoes, okra, green beans and cut up fruit. The President tasted the stake as Mike was coming out of the kitchen. He stood back until everyone got a bite of meat, then came over. "Is that the best steak ever", he said. Everyone was saying how great it tasted and that he did a good job. He walked away so proud with a smile on his face. After lunch, Peter brought the check to me. "I will get that", the President said. "No sir, this one is on me", I said. I gave Mike and Peter a five credit tip and the hostess a two credit tip and we were off back to the conference room.

When we walked into the conference room, it sounded like a mad house but quieted down like a church on Sunday morning. You could hear a pin drop now. Mandy, Judy, and Sunshine were sitting off to the side. The President asked if there were any questions Mr. Anglin or did they need to bring anything else before the committee. No one even whispered. "If everyone is for it, I would like to help Mr. Woods with his problem", I said. "Mr. Woods, if you would set a meeting with the leaders, not the department managers. There are always leaders that speak up for a group. I would like to do this thing at five minutes before 6 AM. I should not take more than thirty minutes. Allow any people coming off shift or people off that day to attend. I was told the theater there will hold about ten thousand people. I do not want any managers nor you present at this meeting. They will trust me better by myself", I said. "I would like to ask if Mr. Bryan would have his people get the template made for the alloy. A six foot by 5 would be nice. If you need help, I would be happy to come down day or night and work on it with you", I said. "We will get it done", he said. "Sunshine has agreed to work on portable generators for me. These generators are real important to the city's health and well-being. I would like to take a generator and let the people know we will be taking care of them", I said.

"If that is all; I will have my managing team and the Governor and LT Governor plan out a new budget for employees and for other essentials you believe we need to get this city on track. I will be leaving on Monday and hopefully we can everything in order", the President said. The President got up with his staff, the Governor and LT Governor and left the room. It got real quiet again. The directors were just sitting there staring at me. I said to have a good day and left the room followed by Mandy. She told me I was seen sitting at the table with the President and that I must be some family member of something. They were afraid to talk. I laughed out loud and everyone close by stared trying to figure out what was funny. Mandy said that since she had to come to the meeting, that she had tomorrow morning off. "How about dinner and dancing tonight I asked. I still need to see Mrs. Wright about her cancer, then I will be right over", I said. As Sunshine was walking away, I told her how beautiful she looked out of coveralls. I think I made her day. She nearly skipped out of the office. Judy said she was going back to the lab smiling at what I told Sunshine.

It was only about 2 PM. I expected the meeting to last a lot longer. I took about fifteen minutes to get to Mr. Wright's house. I was actually nervous about this visit. She had left for home right after lunch. When Marilyn answered the door, she was in a robe. "I was wondering what time you would show up. After yesterday, my pain level was cut in half and I have not been sick all day", she said. "Did you get a scan today", I asked. "No, I am supposed to have one done tomorrow. Are you ready to get started", she said. Marilyn turned and locked the door behind me. I took off my shirt and she dropped her robe. She had shaved off her pubic hair. Even with all the weight she had lost, she was hot. She put her arms around me and hugged. After about five minutes, she turned her head. I could feel her staring at me. I turned my head towards her and she was staring right into my eyes. Her right hand came up my back to my shoulders and her left hand dropped down to my butt. We just stared at each other for a few moments and then she clutched my butt and pulled me into her. Her other hand on my back, she pulled me tight to her as she kissed me. She started motioning her hips as she kissed. "Do you like how I shaved my pussy"? she said as she moved her lips to my neck and then started to lightly lick my neck. Between the licking, the hot breath on my neck and I could feel myself getting turned on. She knew it to. She moved the hand from my butt and undid my pants. When we fell to the floor, she stuck her hand in my underwear and grabbed my hard cock. She then placed one leg behind me and forced me backwards to fall, but I sat on the floor. She then pushed me down and made love to me. She had her pussy in my face rotating it all over. It did not take long for her to orgasm. She shifted and ran my cock in her pussy and pumped like this would be her last ride. She was all over me for about twenty minutes and I could feel her starting to orgasm again. The muscles tightened up inside of her and sucked my cock deep. I could not hold back any longer and started to cum. She started to yell, but somehow held it back. We just laid there for about ten or fifteen minutes. "What time tomorrow", she said. I got up and got dress and she put her robe on. "I don't know my schedule yet. It seems things happen that I cannot organize my time well", I said. I left there and headed home.

On the way I saw Milea and another young lady. "Hi Milea, how are you doing", I asked. I feel so good Mark. I was telling Felicia what you have done for me. We used to be classmates until I had to quit for a while. May I ask you a real big favor Mark?" she said. "I will do anything for you Milea within reason that is", I said. Would you escort me to Felicia's cubicle in the Bulkhead this Saturday? I will only stay a few hours and then you can bring me back", she said. That would be a good chance for me to look around, I thought. "I will be happy to. I need to see Mrs. Wright first that morning about 9 AM and then I can come by and get you if that is okay", I said. "That would be perfect Mark. Thank you, thank you, and thank you", she said. I headed home.

When I got up to the apartment, I noticed the door open. I glanced in and saw Sandra sitting on the couch. I did not have a very good feeling about this, so I went next door to my other apartment. The Jacobs had moved to the other side of the city and I ask Carol to get it for me. I had clothes and everything I need at both apartments. I figured if my mom or a friend were to come by, they could use the apartment. I had more than enough credits to pay for everything. I closed the door and changed my clothes. I was about to leave when I heard someone talking. I saw Mandy at the door talking to Sandra. I could not hear what they were saying, but from the look on Mandy's face, it was not good. Sandra finally closed the door and Mandy went down to the boardwalk. I eased the door open and ran down to the boardwalk. Just as Mandy got around the corner, I caught up with her. She was walking fast. "Mandy", I said. She turned surprised. "What happened back there?" I asked. "Your new girlfriend said she was waiting for you to go dancing, so I left", she said. "I had an uneasy feeling when I saw her in the apartment and made myself scarce. I did not make any plans with her", I said. "Instead of going to the executive dining hall and club, let's find something else to do", I said. "Let's go to my place first", she said. We went to her apartment and once inside turned and kissed me. We held each other for a while and she got dressed and we were out the door. She took me to one of those fast food places that made sandwiches. "I never saw the executive look at you before Mark. You really did stand your ground at that meeting. I was wondering what the President and Governor were going to say", she said. "They really did not say anything. There is always tomorrow", I said. We just sat there for a while talking small talk. "Let's go to the Pub. It is about forty minutes from here. It is not the executive club, but it is not bad", she said.

The club sat back behind some business. It had a big sign, but you could not see it. Maybe I should say something, I thought. We sat at a table across from the band. The band comprised a piano player, drummer, guitar, and bass. They were not very exciting. They had no smiles and no get up and go. Somebody must light a fire under them. I love getting up there and singing. I wonder if I was an entertainer in another life also. "On Friday's and Saturday's they have a large band here. I have never seen these guys before", Mandy said. A waitress walked up to us. "Can I get you something", she said. "Two beers", I said. "I will have them right up for you. I need your card please", the waitress said. A few minutes later she came back with the beers. I pick mine up to sip it. "This beer is ice cold", I said. The owner has some way of cooling them that makes them very cold. May I ask you something? Have we ever met? You look familiar and I never forget a face she said. "I don't remember ever meeting you, I am sorry. My name is Mark and this is Mandy", I said. "My name is Michelle. If you need anything, just yell", she said. A few minutes later Michelle came back. "I remember you. You were talking with the director at manufacturing the other day. You had a little blond girl with you, ah, Sunshine I think her name is. I work at manufacturing then I come here for six hours every evening, but Friday and Saturday. There are four girls that work the weekend in twelve hour shifts. They say they make enough tips to only work two days. That's pretty good isn't. I would have to wait for one of them to die before I got one of their jobs", she said. "Well, we hope no one dies", I said. Mandy just laughed.

I asked Mandy to dance, but this band sounded like something for middle school. If they got any slower, they would fall asleep. We finished the beer and Michelle brought another. "I can't stand this any longer", I said to Mandy. I stood up, grabbed Mandy's hand and beer and headed across the floor. "You guys new at this", I said. "Know, it is just slow tonight", one said. Looking around the room, there were about fifty people. That is a good crowd for a small club. "Let's see if we can perk things up", I said. I picked up the microphone. "There are many things about music. It can bring tears to your heart, laughter, excitement and bring back good memories. Most people come to a club for excitement and laughter. There are some maybe to cry in their beer after losing their best girl. I am Mark Anglin and I think we can liven up this place up" I announced. I even got a few people to clap. I played the piano. "I Am Music and I Write This Song." When I finished people got up and applauded. I went right back into a song that fit Mandy. The song was about a girl named Mandy. People danced and having a good time. "More", they said. The band tried their best to follow with me. They really were not that bad, they just needed rhythm and a pick-me-up. I sang two more songs, then thanked the audience and took Mandy over to a table. "You sing beautiful Mark. I think you can do most anything", Mandy said as she leaned over and kissed me on the cheek. A few minutes later Michelle brought me a few more beers. "On the house from the manager", she said. "Well, tell him thank you very much", I said. "We have not seen people dancing and having a good time like this in years. I hope you come here more often", she said. "Thank you, Michelle", I said. We finished our beers then got up to leave. The people in the club got up and applauded us as we were leaving.

CHAPTER 9 Heaven And Hell

Mandy and I headed back to her place. I wonder if Sandra is still hanging around, I thought. "Are we going to pick up the babies", I asked. I will get them from the Children's Center tomorrow. "I have something I need to ask you", Mandy said. Oh! Oh! I thought. Melissa asked me to talk to you. She wants to have a baby boy and she thinks you are the one to give it to her. She is my best friend, so I told her I would ask" she said. "Wouldn't you think that might cause problems between you and me", I said. "I am fine with it", she said. "I will think about it", I said. We made love for about an hour and fell to sleep sometime in the process. It was close to 7 AM when we awoke being shaken by Melissa. "Did you talk to him", Melissa said. "Yes I did", Mandy said. But before Mandy could actually finished Melissa said she would take a quick shower. "I guess that means I thought about it?" I asked. Mandy just smiled one of those sheepish smiles. A few minutes later, Melissa came out of the bathroom nude. "This is so exciting", she said as she jumped into bed next to me. Mandy and I were still naked from last night. "I guess this means a threesome", I said. Melissa wasted no time coming on to me like a hungry animal. She had an awesome body and knew how to use it. Mandy just laid there and smiled at us. After about thirty minutes, Melissa rolled over huffing and puffing. "This is so good. When can we do it again", she said. "I will have to check my calendar", I said. I got up and got dressed. "I have to get to the lab. I will see you Saturday", I said. When I left, Melissa was squirming around like a little school girl. I just smiled.

"Good morning everyone, Hi Judy", I said as I was walking in the room. I gave Judy a big hug. "Do you know if they had you transferred to me yet? Sounded kind of weird, didn't it?" I said. I hope they can have our room or building ready today. "I want you to stop trying to find a cure for the disease. Doc is going to get someone to take the kids outside on Saturday for a picnic. I will arrange a flatbed and get Big Mike to fix a basket for the kids. I believe being outside will be what the kids need. I am nearly more than positive that Sandra's growth died for being outside." I said. "Speaking of Sandra, she called me last night wanting to know if I had seen you", Judy said. "She was at my apartment when I went home last night, so I made myself scarce. She scares me", I said. "What's going on", she said. "I think us hugging bare has got her thinking about something else other than curing. The last couple of times we met, she kissed me on the lips. That makes it really bad, especially since she is the President's daughter. I am not really afraid of the President, but I really don't want to be fired yet, at least not until I finish what I came here to do. She is very attractive, but also childlike since she has not been around boys or men much because of her illness. I have a problem with Mrs. Wright also. She wants sex every time we start hugging. It is making it really hard to heal her", I said. Judy's face had a big smile and scrunched up face and said, "Marilyn. Oh my God. When did this start?" she said. "She hasn't really said, but she has been hinting about wanting a baby boy. I see her every day. Mandy's friend wants sex to have a boy; now I am in a pickle as to what to do. Any other guy I guess would say he was in heaven. I on the other hand just love you and Mandy", I said. I think, I just stuck my foot in my mouth. "Mandy, um", she said. Maybe I had better change the subject. "I would like to get started on that anti-gravity car. I am going to call it Hover Car", I said. "That's a good name", Judy said. "I will be running around today. I will be going to the Bulkhead area

Saturday. I told Milea I would escort her there to see a friend. I might as well see what damage I can do there." I said.

I headed over to technology. Sunshine was busy going over a bunch of inventory that came in for the generator and the Hover Car. She was all smiles as usual. "I still can't get over yesterday. You are not afraid of anything, are you?" she said. I have inventory here to make at least ten portable generators," she said. Stay on top of manufacturing for me to get those graphluminum sheets going if you will please. Have you heard anything about the building or room I requested Sunshine?" I said. "Not yet boss, but I will keep checking", she said. "I really don't want to start that Hover Car until we have the privacy and room. I would also like to keep us making the portable generators under wrap", I said. "Yea and we need the alloy sheets to finish them up. I am really excited to work with you Mark. If you want me to do anything at all, any time, just let me know. I appreciate all you do Sunshine. "Since I know you will be staying with me, I have a surprise for you. Starting next Friday, you will receive 25,000 credits a month for a year. That should keep you focused. You are to tell no one, not even your mother you are receiving those credits", I said. She looked like I punched her in the chest and took her breath away. "You still excited about working with me Sunshine?" I smiled. "I love working with you. There are a lot of things I could do with that many credits. My family sure can use them", she said. I told her I need to get out of here and if she needed me, I gave her Mandy's number and said she would have to call around if Mandy did not know.

About 11 AM I went by tower. "Hi everyone", I said as I walked in. I was on my way to Carol's desk when Judy, Jerry's secretary stopped me. "Mr. Wright would like to see you Mark", she said. I gave Judy a big hug and knocked on the door and went in. "Hi Mark, I need a few moments with you if you don't mind", he said. He ushered me over to the lounge area. I thought maybe he would say something about yesterday. "Marilyn and I had a long talk about you last night", he said. Suddenly my chair got really hot and uncomfortable. She wants a baby boy and she wants you to get her pregnant", he said squirming a little. "Jerry, do you think that is a good idea? It would probably make you very uncomfortable with someone else making love to your wife and if found out, people may talk", I said. "We considered all that and more last night, Mark. She still wants a baby boy and figures you could deliver. I want to thank you for working with Marilyn also. I know it is tough on you", he said. "I will start stepping up the time spent on her. I need to get her well and not just stop the cancer. It could take weeks or months though. Everyone is different", I said. "Have you heard anything about my request for a building or room so I can start my next project and also the request to have Sunshine and Judy Mimms assigned to me", I said. Judy and Sunshine should already be assigned to you. Human resources were supposed to have everything done this morning. As for the building, Carol found you something. Please check with her Mark. Also please consider what I asked you", he said. "Thank you, Jerry for helping me out. I will talk to you later", I said.

I went over to Carol's desk and gave her a hug. "How is my favorite secretary today", I said. "I heard that", Judy said. "You sure did raise a lot of hell yesterday Mark. The bees are buzzing today. The top brass are impressed with you though", she said. "Did you hear anything on the building I requested", I said. "I have you a building next to manufacturing. That would make it easier for you to get materials and work with Mr. Bryan getting the items manufactured. "I could kiss you Carol. I have a lot of projects that I need to get started on. Some of them will take months or a year or more to complete. I need to get started now.

Question, if I find a person or persons that I believe would be a good fit for what I am doing whether they are corporate or not, do you think it will be hard to get them assigned to my project?" I asked. "After what I heard the President say to Mr. Namor yesterday, you have pretty much free rein. You can do just about anything you want. That is sure going to make most of the directors unhappy", she said. "I will win them over", I said. "I am sure you will Mark. Here are your keys for building 217890. You will need keys and code to open the door", she said. I told her thank you and headed back over the technology. I gave Jodi a real warm hug and asked her for a favor. I told her I need her to get someone to help Sunshine move all the materials in our area to 217890. She said she would and that she was sorry to see us go, but check in on us. I also asked her to see if she could move the phone also. Sunshine was still inventorying in the back. I stopped and told her about the building and that Jodi would get someone to help her. I told her I would try to get back to her this afternoon. I am sure walking a lot today, I thought.

I headed over to Mr. Wright's house. Marilyn was not expecting me this early. "Marilyn, I need to work on healing you, so please hold off on flirting until I am done, please", I said. "Ah, you're no fun today are you", she said. "How were your x-rays yesterday and what level is your pain today?" I said. "My x-rays showed that the cancer had not grown anymore and my pain level right now is about a six. I will not take pain pills for another two hours", she said. She undressed and I had her turn around and pinched her neck. She turned around and we hugged for about ten minutes. I then had her sit in a chair and worked on her head first, using my hands to pull the bad energy from her, then the neck, to the shoulders, down to her stomach and lower back. "How is your pain level now?" I asked. "About a three; can we play now", she asked. My mind fed me information about hypnosis. I must have used it in the other life because I sure did not learn it myself here, I thought. I had her go to the recliner. I told her to lean back and relax and I hypnotized her to focus on her body and get rid of all the rest of the pain. "How is your pain level now?" I asked. "I have no pain at all Mark. You're amazing", she said. "Let me ask you something Marilyn. When making love, have you had more than one or two orgasms in an evening?" I asked. "No, I usually do not have sex long enough to have more", she said. If I could show you how to have four, five, even ten orgasms in one evening, would that interest you?" I said. "I would eat you alive", she said. "Okay, close your eyes again", I said. I hypnotized her to have an orgasm while either kissing, oral or intercourse. She could control when she wanted to have one. Also, each time she had an orgasm with me, it would be more explosive and exciting than any orgasm she had ever had. I told her it was not important that she remember everything that I told her, but her subconscious could take advantage of the affirmations I gave her. I ask her to open her eyes feeling more excited and wonderful about life than she ever felt before. She opened her eyes. "Mark, what did you do? I feel better than I have felt in years", she said. I told her not to forget and get an x-ray done today and that I would see her in the morning and started for the door. "Not so fast. You still have something you need to do. Get naked", she said. She took off the rest of her clothes and went to the bedroom this time. We made love for about an hour. I thought she would never stop. She finally ran out of wind. "I don't remember how many orgasms I had, but it had to be eight or more. I don't think there is a better lover than you in this city", she said. I hurriedly got dressed and left before Jerry got home. Even though he gave me permission, I still would feel very uncomfortable if he walked in.

I went back over to the lab. Judy was working on something using the microscope. "Hey Judy", I said. "Hi Mark", she said. "Will you be ok working with me?" I asked. We have a building number 217890 over by manufacturing", I said. That is good; it is not too far from New City. I want to get an apartment there", she said. I need to tell you something so you don't flip out next Friday. You will receive 25,000 credits once a month for a year. I told you that good things would happen, Judy. Please tell no one you receive that, not even your mother. I already have a bunch of people jealous over what I am doing", I said. "Wow! a brand new wardrobe", she said. "You would look good in anything Judy, even if you just crawled out of a mud hole", I said. "You trying to flirt with me again Mark?" she said. "No, I was just stating the truth. You always look like some type of model or beauty queen", I said. "You already gave me the credits. Do not bribe me", she said. "I wasn't trying to bribe you. I was just stating fact. You have your transfer. When you get over there and see what you need, call the warehouse and tell them to send it over", I said. I left and headed over to the hospital.

I made sure that everything was set for the children to take the picnic trip. I then called to the construction office and made sure the flatbed would be there in the morning. I went to the executive dining facility to make sure Mike would have the picnic food ready for the morning. He said he had a few people that would take care of it. I just hope this field trip works and those children get well.

I headed over to the new building. Sunshine was already in the building putting supplies up. I had drawn out a plan for the building and handed it to Sunshine. The building was completely wide open, so we would have to build different rooms to work out of. The building was 4,900 square feet. I figured we could build eight twenty by twenty square foot rooms and leave the rest wide open. One room I will make a bedroom and have a shower and sink installed. That room can be used in case we work late or all night. I will have one room as an office and drafting room and the rest as storage and work areas. We needed building materials and shelving. I told Sunshine I was going to Broadside sometime in the morning and would not be back until late. I told her I would take Sunday off if everyone lets me sleep in. "Also if Judy comes over today, maybe she can help you some. "You really need to take the weekend off and come back on Monday", I said. "Hey boss, wait a minute. I thought you would like to know I finished the first portable. The next one will look a lot better", she said. "Would you mind if I take this one Sunshine?" I said. "No problem boss", she said. "Thank you again Sunshine, for all you do", I said as walking out the door. I then headed home. I might get a short nap before someone else needs something, I thought. When I got home, no one was there. I had locked the door before I left. When I got inside, I locked the door again. That way no one will know I am home. I called Carol and asked her if she might find me two apartments on the west side closer to where I will work. She said she knew she could if I waited for New City to open up.

I opened my eyes, to knocking at the door. When I opened the door, it was Sandra. What was I thinking opening the door? I rubbed my eyes and said hi. Sandra put her arms around me and gave me a kiss. She hugged me for a moment and said, "I missed you. I waited for you last night, but I guess you were busy working or something." Yea, what can I do for you?" I said. She pushed herself on in and sat down on the couch petting it for me to sit next to her. "I have never made love to anyone before Mark and I want you to be the first", she said with a big smile. "Don't you have a boyfriend back home?" I questioned. "Not really, because I was so sick this last year, I have not got out much. I spent most of my time at the doctor's office. My dad said he is really going to give my doctor a hard time for not finding the cancer", she said. "I want to make love right now and spend the whole evening and night with you", she said. "Does your dad know you are here?" I asked. "He doesn't have to. I am over twenty one and I have a right to do what I want to", she said. "Sandra, would you mind waiting for me for about five minutes? There is something I need to tell my neighbor real quick", I said. I walked out the door and went next door. She was watching for a moment, so I knock. When Sandra went back inside, I used my key. I went straight to the phone and called the operator. "Operator, this is Jill", the person said. "Jill, this is Mark Anglin. Would you please connect me with the President's cubicle?" I asked. "Hi Mark, I saw you sing the other night. You were dreamy", she said. "Thank you, Jill", I said. The phone rang and Mrs. Preston answered the phone. "Mrs. Preston, this is Mark Anglin, would the President happen to be available?" I asked. "One minute Mark", she said. "Hey Mark, what can I do for you", he said. "I have a real problem and I do not know how to handle it. I know you don't think I have a problem talking after the meeting yesterday, but I will try to say this as best I can. I guess the best way is to say it right out. Sandra is in my apartment and she wants to have sex. I don't want to make anyone mad. If I say know to her, she is mad and if I say yes, you and Mrs. Preston are mad", I said. "Mark, you have a real problem there son. The best thing I can tell you is that you can do what you want. She is 21 and able to make up her own mind", he said. "I have two girlfriends already", I said. "You do what you have to do. I will try to back any decision you make", he said. "Okay", I said with hesitation. "Have a good night", he said. "Thank you", I said and hung up.

Damn it is too late to run and hide. Maybe I can talk my way out of this somehow. I went back to my apartment and Sandra was not there. Maybe she left I hoped. "Come here", she said. She was lying across the bedspread naked on her back and legs spread out. This is the first time I had seen her completely naked. She had large breast and a beautiful figure. I was getting turned on just standing there. Well, I stepped into it this time, I thought. I took my clothes off and laid down right next to her. "Being your first time Sandra, you could be so tight you may hurt or bleed", I said. "I have been masturbating with one of those vibrators for about two years. I think I am good", she said. She rolled over and situated herself just over my face. "Lick", she said. She must have read a book or maybe her friends told her how to make love. She was actually good. That took my guilt feeling away for at least a half hour. "That was wonderful Mark. When we get back from dinner and dancing, I want you to make love to me all night long. Let's both take a shower together so we can get done faster", she said. After we got in the shower, she wanted me to fuck her again. She just kept saying fuck me over and over. A little over doing it, I thought. We got dressed and headed to the executive dining facility.

The facility was nearly full. The hostess showed us to a table after giving me a loving hug like she missed me. Sandra's smile disappeared. Just before getting to the table, Peter came up and hugged me. "We have fried catfish", he said with a smile. "That will be fine Peter. Let's see what the lady would like", I said. Peter handed Sandra a menu. "I will have what Mark is having, thank you", she said. A few minutes later Mike came out happy and loud as usual. I stood and he gave me a big bear hug. "You have such a pretty lady", he said. "How is that wonderful family of yours Mike", I said. "They are always wonderful Mark. Little Cathy lost her first tooth last night. She was happy to get a present under her pillow this morning", he said. They are always happy to get a present", I said. "I will make you the best catfish in Texans," he said walking away. "Everyone seems to love you Mark", Sandra said. "Oh, they are all just very nice people", I said. I could see many people quickly looking at us and turning away. I guess we are the talk of the city this evening, I thought. John Cooley and his wife waved. We had basically a quiet dinner with just small talk. Sandra seemed to not have anything in common with me to talk about. After dinner, I made sure I gave everyone their tip and headed with Sandra to the door. Mr. Cooley stopped me. "I am not sure if you knew Kevin Walker. He had been with us since the city started", he said. "No, I am sorry, I don't", I said. Well, he was working on a solar cable not far from Tower. He had his safety harness attached to a dome brace and it gave way and he fell over a thousand feet to his death", he said. "Oh my gosh," Sandra said. "He had a wife and four children", he said. "I appreciate you telling me John. I will make it a point to visit with his family", I said. "Thank you, Mark", he said. "Is it your job to know everyone?" Sandra said. "No, but it would be a good job", I said with a smile.

There must be a thousand plus people in the club tonight. They had a full orchestra and the room was noisy. One of the waitresses gave me a hug and showed us to a table. "Nice crowd", I said. "I love crowds", Sandra said. A few people waved my way. The waitress brought Sandra and I our drinks. "I wish we were closer to the dance floor", Sandra said. "Maybe someone will leave and we can move up", I said. I ask the waitress if she could get us a table closer the dance floor if anyone left. I know most of the songs the orchestra is playing, but I don't like the music much from this world. My other self-had better music, I thought. We were sitting there talking nearly yelling at each other when a man came up next to me. "Our conductor asked if you would come up and sing a song," he said. "Give me a few minutes and I will be happy to", I said. I was thinking this would be a chance to help out Kevin Walkers family. "What about me?" Sandra said. You can come up there with me and sit on the piano bench with me", I said. A few minutes later the conductor made an announcement. A lot of you know Mark Anglin. He has agreed to sing a few songs for us this evening. People applauded. I grabbed Sandra's hand and we walked across the dance floor. On the way to the stage, I ask the waitress if she would get me a pen and paper. The conductor handed me the mic. "Good evening ladies and gentlemen. You know music fills our hearts with laughter, sadness, reminds us of the past and helps us get through a dreary day. This song is about just that. I sang the song "Music, This Is My Song" from my other life. People were not dancing to it, but where catching the beat. I also saw the President and his wife come in and got seated. When I finished, I said I have an announcement. "I know you are here to have a great time, but I need to say something about one of our own that passed away today. Kevin Walker may not have been known by any of you, but he was still part of this city and had been so since this city started. He fell to his death this morning repairing a solar cable to keep the lights on in this wonderful city. We in this city are family and we take care of family. That is what makes a great city. He had a wife and four wonderful children. This lady and her children need our help and our sympathy. I am going to ask all here to pledge one credit, hundred credits or even a thousand credits to help this family in their need. I don't know how to get credits from you to the family, but I am sure someone will figure it out. On this table is a paper. During the next song I would like those who would like to help this family out come up here and put their name and last four digits of their company number on this piece of paper. Any amount would help this family immensely. Also, to put the icing on the cake, I will match any amount pledged tonight. Thank you, ladies and gentlemen. This next song is a song just for this city. The name of the song is "Don't Cry For Me Capital City", I said. I took the song "Don't cry for me Argentina" and changed it. It seemed to work out well. Just before I started singing, someone stands up. "I will pledge

5,000 credits", Mr. Preston said as he headed toward the table. "Thank you, Mr. President", I said and began to sing. People seemed to love the melody and danced. The orchestra was doing a great job staying up with me, for never hearing the song. The floor filled with nearly everyone. People here and there were breaking off and going over to sign the pledge sheet. When I finished singing, the crowd roared. It was like they never heard a great song before. A good many people now were at the table signing their names on the pledge sheet. "I hope I can afford it", I said jokingly. You know there are a lot of people that seemed to think that I get my own way around here. I may not get my own way, but I seem to put myself in a position where it looks that way. So, the next song is dedicated," I said with a smile. I sang the old Frank Sinatra song "My Way." They have never heard of him on this world, now it is time, I thought. The crowd loved it. "I am going to take a break right now. Isn't this a wonderful orchestra?" Please give them a nice big hand. By the way this lovely lady with me tonight is Sandra Preston, I said. Thank you all for coming this evening. Sandra and I walked across the floor with everyone applauding and saying hi. We walked over to Mr. Preston's table. "You sing so beautiful", Mrs. Preston said. "Thank you, ma'am", I said. She was saying something else, but it was hard to hear through all the applauding. "Do you think you can afford this evening", Mr. Preston said. "I am sure I will work it out", I said. "I am sure you will", he said. We spoke here and there. It was really too loud to carry on a conversation. Sandra and I danced and I danced one song with Mrs. Preston. I sang a few more songs and wished everyone goodnight. Sandra and I went back to my place and made love the rest of the evening.

The alarm woke me at 6 AM. I took a shower and got dressed. Sandra was still asleep. I left a note and told her I was going to work and headed over to my new building. There were few people out for Saturday morning. I just love Sunshine. Everything was put away and stacked neatly. I love organization, I thought. The lumber for the walls and rooms had already been delivered. It was still banded but put out of the way. There were about 20 sheets of the alloy stacked in a corner. A portable generator lay close by. What am I doing here? I had no intention of coming in today. I guess my subconscious mind was telling me to get out before I had a problem with Sandra. She really is an alright girl, just not my type.

It was about 7:45 PM and I headed to Jerry's apartment. Marilyn was waiting for me with her robe on. Jerry had gone to play tennis. "I have been waiting for you all night", Marilyn said as I entered the door. "Marilyn, please let's get the healing out of the way first", I said. I spent about twenty to thirty minutes working on her. "I heard you were a big hit last night. Jerry's tennis partner said you raised the roof. I am sorry I missed it" she said. She played with her new ability to control her orgasms. I don't know how many she had, but it was a lot. She tired quickly this morning. "The x-rays yesterday were great. A few of the cancers are receding. The doctor is very happy with my progress. I am very happy with a lot less pain", she said. I left and headed over to Ralf's apartment.

Milea was ready and waiting to go. "That was a good thing you did last night", Ralph said. The President told me this morning. I am supposed to meet him later", he said. "I just want the people of this city working together. Once that happens, we will have a great city, I said. Milea and I headed off down the boardwalk to the Broadside sector.

I really hate this long walk to the south side. Without a car, this city sucks now thinking like the old Mark. Actually my mind is not twirling right now; thinking a hundred things all at once.

Milea was telling me about school. She was so excited to be back in school. She was telling me how she missed her mom. Her dad was now talking to her more which makes her feel a lot less lonely and feeling bad all the time. She was so glad I was her new best friend.

She saw Felicia waiting for her on the boardwalk. They went running at each other like they had not seen each other in years. This area of the city is not kept up like the rest of the city. You would think they would take better care of the place they live. People sometimes just think backwards, I thought. At least they have lights. There were hundreds of people coming through the main entrance to go shopping. "Hi Felicia", I said as I walk up to her. "Hi Mark, I am so excited you came", she said jumping up and down and acting like she had to go pee. "My mom is going to love you all", she said. I saw a florist and I said I wanted to stop. "Hi, I am Madison, how may I help you", the young lady said. "I would like a single rose, with a stem of leather fern, plumosa fern, and baby's breath if possible", I said. "Roses are high right now because of the summer", she said. "That is alright, just wrap it nice, please. Would you also put a water pick on it" I said. "It will be right out", she said. The girls were standing by the door giggling and talking about Felicia's mom, and her brothers. Madison came out with the wrapped rose and a ticket. "That will be 6.95 credits please", she said. I marked 3.05 credits tip and handed it back with 10 credits and my card. She marked the credits and handed me back the card thanking me for such a large tip. "My name is Mark Anglin. Have a wonderful day", I said. "You to sir", she said as we walked out of the store. I handed the rose to Milea. "Give this to Felicia's mom. This will help make her day." I said. We walked for about twenty minutes more, and then started up the staircases. We finally came to Felicia's apartment.

Felicia's mom was at the sink with her back turned when we entered. She had full dark black hair that went down to her lower back. She had one of those most perfect figures like what you would see on a twenty year old. "Mom, this is Milea, that I talk about all the time and this is Mark", she said. Her mom grabbed a hand towel and turned around. She was totally gorgeous. She was more than gorgeous; she was perfect, I thought squirming to get words out of my mouth. Before I could get the words out, she smiled and said, "I am Sarah, nice to meet you Mark and hello there Milea. You are the talk of the city. "As I was holding her hand, looking in gorgeous blue eyes, I said, "It is such a pleasure to meet the most wonderful mom in capital city and by the way you are absolutely stunning." She smiled and asked, "are you Mark Anglin." "Yes I am", I said. "My cousin told me about you. You seem to run the city now according to him. You are always bringing in a new lady to dinner and that you must be a playboy. I also heard you healed Milea and found a cure for that lung disease. You're a little young to have accomplished all that in such a short period of time", she said. "Just luck I guess and who is your cousin", I said. "Mike Reavis, the head chef for the tower", she said. "Mike is a great guy and he cooks nearly as well as my Grandma", I said with a smile. "So Mr. Mark Anglin, come in and make yourself comfortable. The girls will probably be gone for a few hours while Felicia shows Milea off to everyone she meets", she said with the most beautiful smile. Sarah talked about her belated husband, her boys, Felicia and it seemed everything. Actually, she was talking like she never gets company. "Let me ask you something. Do you have any children?" "No, I have never been married. It seems though there are a few here that think I can give them a baby boy though. I think it has a lot to do with the two hundred credits a week you can make." I said. "Yea, I was thinking about that to", she said with a teasing smile. "Well, did you make them pregnant", she asked. "I don't know Sarah, I have only been here two weeks", I said. "Two weeks and you already accomplished what I heard. You must be a really bright young man", she said. We sat there talking small talk for a while and I ask her about how people here in this area felt about the city. She filled me in on most everything she knew or felt.

Sarah then stood up with her hands on her hips like I was about to get chewed out. "I want you to please don't get mad at me. I want to have another baby. My oldest boy turns nineteen soon and I need the extra money coming in. Would you make me pregnant?" she said nearly all in one breath. "Sarah, I do not know what to say", I said. "Please say yes Mark, please." Without saying anything, she just grabbed my hand and ushered me into the bedroom. "The girls won't be back for a while, please", she said. Mark Anglin of two weeks ago would never even had a second thought. In my case, I guess I am a little slow. "The girls won't be back for a while", she said as she unbuttoned her blouse. When her bra fell, I think I started drooling. The most perfect breast I thought. I now could not wait to suck on those nipples. I stripped off my clothes. I have never had women fuck like this one. She knew exactly how to please me. I cummed twice myself. If she were twenty years younger, I would take her home to mom. We laid there for a moment. "You know that there is a fifty/fifty chance that it could be a girl and sometimes it takes more than once to get pregnant", I said. "That is a chance I will gladly take. Will you come back to see me?" She said. We talked for a few more minutes and then got up and dressed. I told her I came up here to speak to people in this district and that I needed to do that before I had to go back.

I walked around for about an hour speaking to people about how they felt about the city and their jobs. Some people were actually happy, some were terribly mad and some would say nothing. I believe they were afraid of reprisals and needed their jobs no matter how bad it was. It gave me something to work with on how to manage talking with the group on Tuesday morning. After a little over an hour I went back to Sarah's. The girls were there talking to Felicia's older brother. I poked my head in the door and said goodbye to Sarah and then to Felecia and her brother and I walked Milea back home. On the way back, I was thinking about all the women in my life the last two weeks. I have been with more women in one day than I have been with in my life. My problem is now the interaction when they see each other and when they see me again. This really was a heavenly week for women and it will probably be hell week facing off this next week.

CHAPTER 10 Another Day

I went back to my place first and took a shower and laid down. Later I woke up and headed over to Mandy's. She wasn't out when Milea and I first past. She was now sitting up on the bleachers with her hands wrapped around her face like the first time I saw her. I sat down next to her and put my arm around her. She turned, smiled and kissed me. "Unless something happens, we can have all tomorrow by ourselves", I said. "I would love that", she said. "Would you like to go to dinner and dancing?" I said. "Wonderful, I will get changed, she said. We went up to her apartment and she went into the bedroom and came out with two dresses. "Which one", she said. "You would look gorgeous in either one. The blue one would be fine", I said. She changed quickly and we were off to the Tower. As we entered the dining hall, people were saying hi, waving or nodding their head. "You're getting popular", Mandy said as we were being seated. "Good evening Mark. I hope you and the lovely lady are having a nice evening", Peter said. "I would like a thick steak grilled, burnt on the outside and pink on the inside, French fries, green beans if available and some kind of mixed fruit if possible and whatever Mandy would like", I said. "I would like a small piece of baked chicken, rice, fruit and a small salad", she said.

"Are you going to heal the rest of those children?" Mandy said. "I am hoping the outing outside will kill the growth in their lungs and I am able to possibly heal them all in one day sometime later this week", I said. "You have accomplished a lot since you have been here this week", she said. "I will have another real busy week this week, especially with the service people. I am not sure how much I will see you through the week. I would like to take you somewhere Friday or Saturday though", I said. "Where to?" she asked. "I am not telling you. You will just have to think about it all week and probably bug the hell out of me", I said. John Cooley then stood up. "I would like to say something. As you know one of my employees Kevin Walker fell to his death the other day. Well Mark Anglin asked the citizens of this city to help out his family. There was over a 100,000 credits raised by the citizens and Mark said he would match whatever they donated. That is over 200,000 credits. No one in the five years since I have been in this city has done anything like that for one of the citizens here. I would like to commend him and thank him for all he has done. Thank you Mark", he said. People stood and applauded. I just thanked everyone and Mandy and I left for the executives club. The place was packed but, I had reserved a table. I had a table reserved just to the right of the orchestra, between the orchestra and the bar. That way I would not have to cross the dance floor to get to the orchestra when they ask me to sing again. I ordered two beers. The beers here were not as cold as the Pub. I was wondering how they cooled their beverages. The conductor asked me to sing and I first sang the song "Don't Cry for Me Capital City." They love that song. I sang a few other songs and then took a break. I danced about four songs with Mandy and noticed the President, wife and daughter being seated. I really need to go say hi, but I really don't want to face Sandra. I sang a few more songs and danced a few, then sat down. I was procrastinating going over there. The waitress brought two beers and said they were from the President's table. "I guess we need to take a walk over to the President's table", I said reluctantly. "I hope he doesn't ask me to work tomorrow", I said. Mandy and I stood up when the orchestra started the next song and danced. We worked our way to the other side of the dance floor when the orchestra stopped. "Thank you for the beers", I said as I approached the Presidents table. "You're very welcome. I hope you two are having a pleasant evening", he said. "Mandy, you have already met the President, this is his lovely wife and daughter, Mrs. Preston and Sandra", I said. "I am pleased to meet you", Mandy said. I could hear Sandra mumble something. "I would like you to meet me at the Tower about 7:30 AM Monday if you will before I leave. I have a few things to go over with you", he said. "It will be my pleasure Mr. President", I said. "Now, you two go have some fun and I will see you later", he said. Mandy and I went back to our table. I sang a few more songs and we danced more and then I took Mandy home.

Just as we got to the front door I said, "Maybe we should have gone to my place. Do you think Melissa is here?" "Melissa is my best friend and she is so lonely", Mandy said. Mandy opened the door and Melissa was sitting on the couch with her robe on. "Hi, you two. Did you have fun tonight?" she said. "We had a great time Mandy", said. "I have been waiting like forever", she said. We all went to bed. The next morning, the alarm went off at 4 AM. Mandy forgot to change it. We went back to sleep. I awoke about 7 AM, laid there for a while, then got up. Both girls stopped me and said we needed to sleep in this morning. We slept little though. Finally about 10:30 AM we got up. Melissa went to the Children's Center to get the girls. Mandy and I sat outside talking. We both talked at the same time. Mandy told me to go ahead. Mandy, I believe you love me. I love you to, but I have no plans of marriage. I don't know the best way to say this without sounding crazy. I believe I have up to ten years to do everything that I need to get done. After that, I don't know if I will be dead or if I will be just the same old Mark Anglin I was two weeks ago before I came. I am also in love with Judy, but it seems I like you more. They have been talking about me being breeding stock to possibly get many girls pregnant, hopefully with a baby boy. I have also been pulled into sex with some other women. I don't want to be unfaithful, but that is how it is. I just thought it would be fair if you knew. If you want to quit seeing me, I will understand", I said. "I am pregnant. I don't know if it is a boy or girl, but I am pregnant. If it is a boy, the city will pay me an extra 200 credits which I could really use", she smiled. "I am so very happy for you. You will probably not need the 200 credits a week though. Starting next Friday, you will receive 25,000 a month for one year. That should help you a lot. I have more good news for you. By next year, they should have the medical school set up. You will be allowed to go to school to be a doctor. It will not cost you anything. You will go to school and still work. Also, if you want to move to New City, I can get you a two bedroom apartment there. I can also get one for Melissa right next door if you like", I said. "Is this a bribe not to see me again", she said. "No, I still want to see you. You are in the right place at the right time. I still want to take you some place next weekend if you are up for it", I said. Mark, I will do whatever you want as long as I can be with you", she said with a tear in her eyes. I need to find someone for Melissa", I said. Mandy, I will not be seeing you all week, because I have so much going on. I need to be on my toes", I said. "Okay Mark", she said.

Melissa came back and we put the babies in their buggies and we just walked to the south. I have never been past the Tower to the south. An area looked like it could handle another new part of the city and more. My mind just began clicking again thinking of all the things I could do with it. We found a place to eat and rest and headed back. About 5 PM, I told the girls goodbye and headed over to Mrs. Wright's. Even though I enjoyed the sex, it just did not feel right going over there. When I knocked on the door Jerry answered and invited me in. "Did you think about what I said?" Jerry said. "I will do it", I said. "Let me get out of here and find something to do", he said hurriedly leaving. "I wondered if you were coming today Mark. I thought you might skip out because of Sunday", Marilyn Said. She was standing there totally nude. I guess she heard Jerry and I talking at the door. I worked on her for about twenty minutes until the pain got unbearable. "My pain level was down today", she said. She took my hand and we went to the bedroom. A guess she was trying something new. At first we just laid there on our sides facing each other with me inside her. She pulled me close and just laid there. I was about to fall asleep when she rolled me over and got on top. We made love for only about thirty or forty minutes. She had some pains in the area around the left breast. We stopped and I used my energy on it until the pain went away. "I hope I see you tomorrow", she said. I got up, dressed and headed back to my place. I would have a heavy day tomorrow. I was taking a hot shower when Melissa stuck her head in. "Room for one more", she said as she climbed in. I told her I needed to get rest tonight. She just ignored what I was saying and played with me. After a long shower, we got out and dried. I told her to go home. She finally left like a whipped dog.

I got to the office little after 7 AM. Carol and another lady were the only ones there. I gave Carol a hug and sat down by her desk. "Here is your pay stub from last week", she said. "I did not know I was getting paid", I said. "By the way, that office over there is yours and so is your new secretary. She thinks she is some pretty hot stuff. She is from corporate", Carol said. "I don't need an office. Thank you Carol", I said as I was walking across the office area.

"Good morning Mr. Anglin. I am Dawn", she said. "Carol says you are from Corporate. I hope you were nice to Carol. She is one of my closes friends" I said. She shifted in her chair a little. "Why did corporate send you to me?" I asked. "I am a specialist", she said. "What is your specialty", I said. "I am an executive's secretary. I can handle anything that you need me to do. I report directly to you and no one else", she said. "I don't know how that makes you a specialist, but okay. Nice to meet you Dawn, I said as I walked into my new office. It was as nice as the Governor's office. I sat down at the desk and opened the envelope. One million credits. I wonder what that is all about, I thought. I went to the door and ask Dawn if the President had come in yet. "Not yet sir, she said with a smile. I was a little worried about coming up with that 107,000 credits for the family of the man who died. A few minutes late, Dawn buzzed me that the President had come in. I went directly to his office. "Good morning Mark", he said. "Did you give me these credits for healing your daughter? I do not accept money for healing anyone" I said. "That is what the board of directors thought you were worth. Also, you have been put in charge of a lot of things you did not ask for. Being a corporate executive under me, you can pretty much write your own ticket. You can go into any city in this state and take charge if you felt the need. The Governor and LT Governor are well aware of what has taken place. Just make me proud", he said as he sat down. With mouth open, I did not know what to think. "I did not mean to stun you Mark", he said. "I did not come to this city for fortune or fame. I came here to just help people. Now the opposite has occurred." I said. "We do not know actually who you are or where you came from, but we do know that you have the knowledge and know-how of someone much older than yourself. You have proven to be one of the most valuable people in this Corporation. After listening to you talk Thursday, I nearly gave you this city. You not only inspired me, but you inspired everyone at that meeting whether they wanted to admit it or not. "Thank you, sir", I said. "One of the first times you have little to say", he laughed. "This is why I wanted to speak with you today. Oh, and by the way, thank you for not being hard on Sandra", he said. "Sandra is not as naïve as you may think Mr. President", I said. "I know she gets around. Her mother knows what is going on more than I do. I need to get on the road. I will come back this way to check on your progress. If this week is anything like the first week, the next month should be outstanding", he said. We shook hands and he left. I went back to my office and ask Dawn to come in.

"You will notice Dawn that I hug a lot. It makes me feel good and I hope it makes the other person feel good. I don't do it for favors or for flirting", I said. "Yes sir", she said. Dawn was really a striking lady. She was about thirty with full brown hair.

Her makeup was on perfect. She wore a business dress with high hills. She was one of those ladies that had legs all the way to her neck it seemed. I have a real busy day and since you have been assigned to me, I will make you busy as well. I need you to first get a hold of Director Woods and ask him when I can see him. He will be all the way to the south, so it will take a while for him to get here. Second, I need Director Bryan when possible this morning. If he is in his office, tell him I need to see him now, please", I said. I pulled out a notebook from the desk and started sketching.

There was knocking at the door and Director Bryan entered. What can I do for you Mr. Anglin", he said. "Please call me Mark", I said. "Is it true that you are now a corporate executive", he said. "It looks that way. I need to know what you are working on now and what are your priorities Kelly?" I asked. "Our main priority right now is the furniture for New City", he said. "How many generators have you completed?" I asked. "We made eleven, but the President had five of them sent to Paso and one to Antonio City", he said. Can you give me an estimate of how long and how many personal it takes to build a flat truck?" I asked. We could build a flat truck in a day with six people working on it. "I know you're not going to like this Kelly. I need you to pull people from the furniture and put them on the generators, buses and ambulances. I will also need a small generator, smaller than the one I brought to the meeting. I need an electric bus something like this, showing him the sketch I made. I need about 40 built. I need you to use your imagination and make the vehicle to handle as many passengers as possible. I know this will delay New City, but we need these items soon", I said. "I need more personnel. Where am I suppose the get them? I need to appropriate more money and that will take time with the corporation", he said. "I will get you a million credits to start. You will have all the credits you need when you need it. I will also need vending machines made that will give credit coins for people using the bus. You will need to create a coin that will be worth 1.5 credits. I will try to recruit this week for more personnel for you and other departments. I also need to see if you can put a break in the dome close to manufacturing", I said. "If you can do all that Mark, I apologize for ever standing against you", he said. "One more thing Kelly, I will have a large deck built in that area north of you for manufacturing. It will not be covered. It can be used for manufacturing and for parking the buses. I will order the lumber tomorrow. We are going have a bus line now in the city to help get our citizens around and improve shopping for the outsiders coming in.

We need to get this city moving", I said. Kelly left the office, not complaining, but running figures on how to organize it. Mr. Woods on the phone Dawn said over the intercom. Billy, just following up, we will have the meeting set for about 6 AM. You will not attend nor will the managers. I need to see the Mayor of the area, the leaders and anyone who wants to show up coming out of their shifts. People going on their shifts should be at work on time", I said. "You are all set for the convention center", he said. "I appreciate your time Billy", I said. "Dawn, I need to see the Director of Housing also please", I said. "Right away", she said. About twenty minutes had past and the Director of Housing came in. She was an older lady with white hair and a stern looking face. I better pay my rent on time, I laughed to myself.

"Ms. Weis, I am Mark Anglin. I thought we should meet", I said. "I have heard good things about you Mr. Anglin", she said. "Please call me Mark. I need to ask you something. There are 40 floors in this tower. I know what is on floors 1, 2, 3,37 ,15, 39 and 40 are being used for. What I would like to know is what are on the other floors? I was told they are executive offices and no one goes there. I see people coming and going, but never see the people that work in those offices", I said. "I was told when the tower was built, that those floors were off limits, so I have never seen them", she said. "Let's take a trip, I said as I picked up a notebook. I want to see these offices. The club was on the 40th floor and we were on 39. We started on 38. The elevator door opened to an empty office. It was fully furnished, but had never been used. We went to the next floor. There were about 75 secretaries working at different stations. Only one office from the main floor was being used by the head secretary I guess. Floor 36 was also empty, as were floors 35 to 16 were also empty. 15 was the Executive Dining. 14 to 4 were also empty. 3 was being used by Human Resources and 2 was being used by Housing and Commercial Rentals. "33 offices are vacant. Can you explain why no one has ever said anything about this or had even an inkling of the vacant offices?" I said. "No, you will have to talk to the governor", she said. I let her out at floor 2 and went back up. "Carol, is the Governor in?" I asked. "Yes sir", she said as she buzzed him. "Go right in Mark", she said. "Hi Mark, you enjoying your new title", I really have not had time to think about the new title. Governor, are you aware that we have 33 vacant floors in this tower?" I said. "No, all floors should be utilized by our people or the corporate people", he said. "I just inspected the floors and it looks like there have never been anyone utilizing those offices", I said. "We were told to stay off those floors when the tower was built", he said. I would like to utilize those floors. I will contact the President and let him know what I am doing just in case he has them earmarked for something", I said "Corporate keeps us in the dark about a lot of things Mark. We just follow protocol", he said. "Are you aware of the power that was handed down to me by corporate sir?" I said. I know you have the leverage to do just about what you want in any city", he said. "I have unlimited resources. The President wants to use this city as a model city. If you have a few minutes, let me give you a layout of what I planned for this week. I will have manufacturing build me 40 buses to be used to transport citizens and visitors around the city. I am having 1.5 credit coins made up to be used for ridding the buses. This will hopefully get more people shopping throughout the city rather than at the entrances only. I will have 12 ambulances made so we can get people to the hospital faster. I will have a deck built by manufacturing they can use in manufacturing and parking of the 40 buses when not in use. I plan to do some recruiting starting tomorrow afternoon. I will offer a bonus if a person stays with us one year of one month's credits. Hopefully, I will have time in between to get with Betty Morgan to work on trying to attract people for the University", I said. "That is a lot to accomplish in a week", he said. "I may not get it all done this week, but I will have it started. We just have to get this city moving", I said. "You are doing a great job Mark. I just have not figured out how you know so much about so many things. I know you do not have to, but please keep me up to date on your progress Mark", he said. We spoke for a few more minutes and I went back to my office.

"Dawn, question; are you sending in a report to corporate on everything I do here?" I said. The President told me that I had to. They want to keep an eye on you", she said. "Before you send any report in, I would like to see it first. Just a heads up if you file a report without my knowledge and I find out, you will be on your way back to corporate", I said firmly. "Yes Sir", she said. "I will be going over to the hospital and then down to my technology building. This is the number for the tech building if you need to get a hold of me", I said.

I left the Tower and headed over to the hospital. Doc was supposed to have a few girls there for me to heal. Then I headed to the tech building. Judy and Sunshine were busy working on the Hover Car. I gave both girls a big hug. "I am right where I really did not want to be. I am now a corporate executive and have command over most of corporate assets. I can even tell the Governor what to do", I said. "I need you two to start building some small generators. I want to use them in the buses I have planned. I am going to try to get us another person in here to help out. Tomorrow I would like to take you with me Judy to that 6 AM meeting and then go outside to meet with some people. I wish I could take you to Sunshine", I said. I would love to go. I haven't been out of this city in years", Judy said. Remember, everything we do in here is confidential, even to the Governor. I arranged for a flat cart to pick us up just outside my place", I said. Let's break for lunch. My treat at the executive dining hall", I said. "I am not really dressed for the executive dining hall", Sunshine said. "You look beautiful as always Sunshine, let's go", I said. We had lunch and the girls went back to work and I went back to the office.

Dawn was busy doing whatever. She seemed very efficient. "Dawn, would you get me Betty Morgan, the education director", I said. I walked into the office and before I had a chance to sit,

Dawn buzzed me that the director was on the phone. "Betty, how are you today. I really need to sit down with you and possibly some of your colleagues to discuss recruiting for the University. Could we meet today?" I asked. "I can be there in about twenty minutes", she said. I buzzed Dawn to get hold of the President. A few minutes later she buzzed me. I asked the President about the empty floors. He was not aware they were earmarked for anything. I told him I wanted to use those floors for University classes. He thought that was a good idea. You could tell from his voice he was upset about the empty floors "Dawn would you try to get a hold of someone in charge of the medical school in Antonio, please?" I asked. A few minutes later she had a Doctor Zorgen on the phone. I explained to him what I was trying to do. He said he could give me a few people to help in organizing the class structure. Everything seemed to fall in place. No stumbling blocks yet. A few minutes later Betty came in and we sat and discussed recruiting for the University and the technical school. I told her about the floors here at Tower she can use. She was thrilled to death. She was worried it was going to take too long to build class rooms. We discussed Antonio City sending over some Doctors to help get her medical school started. After about four hours, she left. I gave Dawn a big hug and told her I would be gone until the day after tomorrow, that I would leave the city to get lumber and hopefully recruit a few new people to help me out. I told everyone bye and I headed over to Mrs. Wright. I did the healing and we had sex as usual, and then headed home.

I called Judy about 5 PM. She was just getting ready to leave. I ask if she would like to have dinner with me. She agreed and I went over to her apartment and we went to the Executive Dining facility. She said it would make it a lot easier if I stayed at your place tonight. After dinner, we went back to her place and she packed a few things and we headed back to my place. We made love for a short while. I reminded her that 3 AM comes early.

CHAPTER 11   A Day Of Sunshine

It felt like we just went to sleep when the alarm went off. Judy took a shower first. A few minutes later she came out drying her hair. I just could not help myself drooling at the sight of her body. Everything about her was just so beautiful. She noticed me staring and smiled. The flat truck was waiting for us as promised. It sure made life easier to have a ride. When we got there, there must have been five or six thousand people there. There was a mic on the stage. I took the mic and sat down on the stage. "Good morning ladies and gentlemen", I said. "I am not a gentleman", a voice rang out. "My grandma taught me to say ladies and gentlemen as a sign of respect. If you find out differently, then you can call them anything you want", I said. "You going to feed us a lot of BS again?" another voice asked. "If you would just hold it down and let me talk and you can ask questions after. First of all, my name is Mark Anglin. About two weeks ago I was living in Ktown, working for a cedar mill that furnished the lumber for this city. So I am pretty much one of you. I know most of you worked for a business or had your own business and along came the big corporate stores and ran you out of business or cost you your jobs, then had to end up working for the man to feed your families. I volunteered to come here and talk to you because I am one of you. We need to get the citizens in this city working together like family. That means not only the service people, but the manufacturing, health, science and technology and the corporate people. We are getting ready to make a great many changes that are going to affect every citizen in Capital City. What I would like is to get everyone in service to come up with a list of complaints you all have. Give your list to your leaders. They will go through them and weed out duplicates and complaints that need not be on the list", I said. "How about getting rid of the twelve hour days", a voice said. "That I can't promise", I said. I would also like to see a list of what you think would improve your job. What you think we need to improve our city. You know your job better than anyone. Tell us or show us what we need to do to make your job more efficient. If you could get up in the morning and tell your spouse; I will see you later. This will be a great day. I just love this job. And when you come home you say, honey, I had a great day. See how great that board walk is. I did a great job today or possibly I cooked a meal today I believe everyone will remember forever. Bottom line ladies and gentlemen, if you are happy, you work better and you become more efficient", I said. "What about the electricity", one person yelled. I have something to show you. We will be hooking up larger versions of this next week. Let me show you how it works. Judy plugged the unit into the wall and the electricity got bright. This generator is self-sufficient. Cloudy days, will not affect the lighting what so ever. You will notice it increase the lighting throughout the center here. If you were to go outside, you would see the lights around also are brighter. The units we will be placing in the part of the city will be about four foot tall and three foot diameter. You will get the first units out of production sometime next week. There is another change you should be aware of. You know in the past the corporation fired no one. They would just place a person in the worst job hoping they would quit. That will not happen anymore. Now the person will be fired and not allowed to come back to the city any more. You know as a family, you try to help someone when they are down. Help them make up for lost work. Also with a large family, it seems you always have a black sheep. A person that complains all the time that sponges off of everyone and just won't get off his or her butt to work. Those people infect the rest of the family and will no longer be able to stay", I said "I will vouch for Mark", a voice rang out. I know he is a good man and he has helped many people the last few weeks. He is also the one that made that generator", he said. I see Big Mike walking up to the stage. "You people know me and I have never steered anyone wrong. This man will do what he can to make it right for you", he said. "I will stand by him", I heard Sarah yell out. People talked between themselves getting louder and louder. Finally a man from the front roll stood up and said that we will take everything you have said under consideration. We will get your list and see if you will do what you say. "You will be able to take time from your work to get the list done. Would Friday be a good time to pick up the list?" I said. "Friday will be good", he said. Judy and I talked with the people after the meeting. Sarah came up to say hi. "Sarah, this Judy", I said. "Nice to meet you Judy," Sarah said. "Sarah, I want you to take this generator and plug it in at your place until the new generators get in place. This will at least assure you and a few apartments around you electricity", I said. "I need to talk to you when you come back", Sarah said. "I will get with you on Friday if that is alright", I said. Judy and I left and headed for the city entrance.

There was not a cloud in the sky. It felt like about 100 degrees. The city stays about 77 degrees all the time, so this is a big change for us. It took about twenty minutes to get to my Bronco and we were off. Judy was like a little kid, noticing everything. I think she saw every flower and tree that had blooms. Every bird that flew by was cute, even the buzzards. She saw a deer by some trees and asked me to stop. This may be a long trip I thought. We finally got to the road leading to Ktown. About five miles out of Ktown, I pulled into the Cedar Mill. I pulled up to the shack. I was just about to open the door and Jordan came out. "Hi boss. I need to discuss something with you", I said. "You want your job back", he said. "No, no not that", I said. "By the way Jordan this is Judy", I said. "You were always one to pick the prettiest girls around Mark", he said. "You told me that you were going to lease another five thousand acres of cedar. I have a proposition for you. I need one hundred thousand square feet of half inch by six to eight foot cedar boards and a million running feet of two by twelve or two by ten cedar boards for Capital City." "You're kidding right", he said. "No, and I need it as soon as it can be milled. Do you think you can hire the people to get it done or should I see if another mill can take part of it", I said. "I would need to bring in about fifty more guys, but yes I can do it. How is the corporation going to pay? I hope it is not ninety days again", he said. "Jordan, go to the bank with me and we will get this sorted out now so you know exactly how you stand. Jordan got in the back seat of the Bronco and we drove to Corporate Bank. They have the only banks in this state. "I need to see the president or vice-president I said as we entered the bank. I have a multi-million dollar deal I need to address. The lady took me to the President's office. "Good morning, I am Mark Anglin, this is Judy and I believe you know Jordan here", I said. "Yea, Jordan and I go back to the old school days. It is nice to meet you Judy and Mark. What can I do for you? I need to set up a payment schedule for Jordan's mill. This is my executive card. I handed him the card. I need for you to transfer 100,000 credits to his account today. I will also need you to transfer to his account credits for lumber delivered. He will bring you the signed receipt after delivery", I said. You have a clearance ten Mr. Anglin. I will get right to it. If you need anything, this is my card. I am always ready to help. Please give my regards to the President", he said. Well, that was easy I thought. "I am impressed Mark. What did you do to get so high on the food chain?" Jordan said. "Just fell into it", I said. "I bet", he said. "Jordan, the delivery will be on the west side of the city.

There will be flags to mark the area. I need the two by twelve's or two by tens first", I said. We spoke for a moment more then I said I had to get going. We still needed to go to Waco today. We took Jordan back to the mill.

We headed over to Josh's office first. Josh was a friend back from school and he ran a contracting company. He employed about ten guys. I told Judy I would try to hire him. It took about ten minutes to get there. Josh was outside talking to some of his men. "Hi Josh, this is Judy", I said. "Wow, you certainly hooked a pretty one Mark. What can I do for you", he said. "I work with Capital City now and we are looking for good people. I would like to talk to you about coming to work for the city", I said. "Well, the construction business has been dropping off. I was just telling some of my guys that I might have to cut someone. What are they offering?" he asked. 7,000 credits for you and 4,000 for your guys and you will also receive a bonus if you stay with the city for one year of one month's credits", I said. "I probably make more than 7,000 now but how long will it last? My guys are not making 4,000 now and would jump on it. When would I have to let you know," he said. "I need people as soon as possible", I said. I have 11 guys and I might be able to pick up 8 or 10 more if you need them", he said. "I need as many people as possible who can handle a hammer. Just report to the Human Resources at the tower when you get there", I said. "Have you seen Rocky?" I asked. "I saw him yesterday, he is still over on 2nd avenue", he said. We said our goodbyes and headed over to Rocky's. Rocky and I played ball together in high school. He is an electrical contractor. "Hey Rocky", I said as I walked up to him. He grabbed me and just hugged and would not let go. It is good to see you buddy", he said. "This is Judy", I said. "Man, please tell me I can take her home", he said laughing. "What's up, he said. "I work for Capital City and I am out trying to find help. I need electrical, construction, workers of all kinds. I would be interested in hiring you. You would work directly with me. The pay for you is 7,000 credits and any of your guys that come along 4,000. Also at the end of the first year you would receive one month's credits as a bonus. Yea man, business is down. I would be very interested. Would my guys be working with us?," he said. "No, they would go out to other divisions of the city", I said. "When do you want us to report?" he said. "Whenever you can. How many men do you have?" I asked. I have six, but I can probably get a few more. Jobs are scarce right now. I need people with experience for the 4,000 credits. If they don't have experience, they will get 3,000 and still be eligible for the bonus after one year. Go to the Human Resources at the Tower when you get there", I said.

We left there and headed for my moms. She was at the flower shop snacking. She never stopped long for lunch. "Hi mom", I said. "Well, will wonders never cease? I was wondering how long you would last working for that city", she said. "This is Judy", I said. "You're very pretty. I hope he is taking good care of you", she said. "Mom, we just needed to lie down for maybe an hour. We have been up since 3AM. We still must go to Waco and back to Capital City", I said. "Why don't you lie down Mark and I will sit and chat with your mom for a moment", Judy said. "I don't know whether that is safe or not", I said. I left and went to the house to lie down.

"Mark, let's go Mark", Judy was saying as she was shaking me. I rubbed my eyes and. I don't think an hour was enough. We went back over to the flower shop and I kissed my mom goodbye and we headed to Waco. "What did my mom and you have to talk about?" I said. "Oh, not much, just ladies talk", she said. I just let it go. It seemed she was not talking. Judy was still looking at everything as we were driving down the road to Waco. After about an hour, we stopped at a lake. Judy's eyes just lit up when we came up to it. "I have only seen one lake before", she said. I pulled into a park and drove down to the edge of the water. "Let's stop and watch the water for a while", I said. She jumped out and ran to the water, splashing it up and telling me everything about the lake. She was like a child in a way. She is so beautiful and so happy right now. I really hate to ruin the mode. I went to the Bronco and got a blanket I brought from the house. We just laid there talking, kissing and looking at the water. After a while, we loaded up and headed to Waco.

I found the local newspaper office after searching for about thirty minutes. "We would like to place an ad", I told the lady. "What size and write an example for me please", she said. I wrote her what I wanted and a somewhat picture of the city and told her full page Friday, Saturday, and Sunday. "We have a picture of the city", she said as she went over the sketch. "Are you a corporate office or free office?" I asked. We are a free office", the cost is 3,750 dollars", she said. Looking behind her I see a map of North America. "Could I possibly get a copy of that map?" I said. "It will be a few minutes. That is oversize paper", she said. She came back with the map rolled up. That will be 3,810 dollars", she said. I pulled the cash from my pocket and thanked her. We then headed south to Tembel. I stopped at the bank and got more cash from my executive card before going to the newspaper. It was also a free paper, but cost less for three days running. We then headed back to Capital City. Judy was constantly sexually teasing me all the back to Capital City. I was just about to make the turn to the city and decided to go straight ahead. We drove into Austin, the old capital city and down to the Nevada River. Next to the river was a real nice motel by the water. I pulled in. Judy had fallen asleep, so loudly I announced we are home. When she opened her eyes she smiled, laughed and stood there like she needed to pee or something. We went in and registered. This was a Corporate Hotel, so I put it on my executive card. I took her bag up to the room. She was so thrilled. We had a great view of the lake. The city across the water looked pretty nice. We could see a few boats on the water. Later we went down to the restaurant and order food. I ordered a bottle of red wine to go with the dinner. We had dinner on the balcony with the nice south breeze from the lake blowing against us. The lights came on and we ordered another bottle of wine and just sat there and talked for hours. "I have never done anything like this. Let's go to the room", she said. When we got to the room, we looked around. We never looked at the room when we first came here. The bath tub was one of those deep tubs with air jets. I have seen them in books, but never been in one. I have always wanted a shower with water jets hitting you all over, I thought. "Let's take a bath", now she said. She turned on the water and we hurriedly stripped. Judy had found candles and a lighter. She lit the candles and turned out the lights. This was nice, I thought. We played and made love in the tub for about an hour. We then sat by the window, looking at the glow of lights on the water for a while.

We did not set an alarm. It was 9:18 AM when I woke up. We need to get going Judy", I said. I nudged her, but she seemed to take her time getting up. She is so beautiful lying there nude on the sheets. Judy rose up and gave me a lovingly soft hug. "I love you", she said. That made me wish we didn't have to go back. It did not take long for us to be back on the road. I had a lot to do and it did not seem like I had enough time to do everything. It did not take long and we were back at Capital City. There were a large number of people going in and out doing their shopping. Judy went to the west and I took the boardwalk to the east. While walking I am looking at how many feet between the railing and the buildings. It was about thirty feet. Figure six feet for the buses on each side. I know I could make this work I said to myself. We will need at least ten buses going all the way around, going and coming. We have four boardwalks that split the city from east to west. Four on each, sixteen plus the sixteen; thirty six would be a good start. I got to my place and changed. I then headed to the tower.

"Hi everyone", I said as I entered the office. "Have a nice vacation?" Carol said. "It was all work", I said. I gave Dawn a hug that took her off her feet. She was still hugging like a stiff board. "You have to relax", I said. "I need to see the following people, please. First Sharon Riggs, Sonia Weis and then John Ryan Please", I said.

Sharon was one of the nervous people that seemed afraid of everything. She came into my office like she was going to get whipped. "Good morning Sharon. May I ask you a personal question? How did you land the job of Director?" I asked. "I am the Governor's sister, sister-in-laws aunt", she said. "I would like to hypnotize you to be more aggressive. Would you agree to that?" I said. She shook her head and I did about a 15 minute hypnosis on her. Her face completely changed from meek to more business-like. "Now I want you to practice looking at yourself in the mirror every day and keep telling yourself, I am becoming more and more aggressive", I said. "I will do just that sir", she agreed. I need you to start hiring as many people as we can get. I would rather have people with job experience, but if not, we could use them in service. I have already contacted 15 to 20 contractors and electricians to come in. Please write this down. There will be one man named Jim Peters who I want to hire as a supervisor and a guy called Rocky who I want him assigned at my building. I need at least two electricians to go to utilities. The rest assign to Building. Any people you see that seem to have a high IQ please flag and I will talk to them later. Jim Peters and Josh Winters will start at 7,000 credits. Those others with experience will start at 4,000 credits and the rest at

3,000 credits. Flag all new recruits coming in that they will receive one month bonus at the end of one year. Do you have that?" I asked. "What about budget?" she asked. "No budget, just hire as many people as we can get. We will worry about budget later", I said.

I am sitting here wondering if all these Directors are kin to someone higher up. Sonia came in all business like. "What can I do for you Mr. Anglin?" she said. I need you to transfer service employees working in Broadside to New City. We will have several new employees. Please try to billet them as close to work as possible. Please work closely with Sharon", I said.

John Ryan will not be happy with me. I just hope I can turn him around. John came in with clip board in hand slamming around. "We are going to have a lot of work to do and I need it done yesterday", I said. I knew that would set him off. I smiled to myself. "What have you set me up for now", he said. I need you to pick one of your people that is a good leader and knows building. I want to make him a Director in charge of building and repairs. I am taking repairs away from services and planning on taking smaller jobs away from you. You will be Director of Construction. You will get new people soon. One I know does a good job building homes and commercial buildings. I just ordered a ton of lumber to come in soon to build a deck just north of manufacturing to be used for manufacturing. We don't have time for a building, so I just want a deck about 100,000 square feet. We will make a hole in the dome to allow the lumber to come in there. The other products needed to build the deck are in manufacturing. I am not worried about cost right now. We have projects we need done soon", I said. "I would still like to know who you really are, for someone to come in here as you have and take over in just couple of weeks", he said. By the way, this does not mean you can keep all your personnel you have right now. I will need some of your people to go over to Building and Repairs. Filter out the people with the least experience to go there. I will need the name of the person you chose for director on my desk in the morning, please. I appreciate your time. Have a good day", I said.

I buzzed Dawn. "Dawn is the Governor in?" I asked. "Yes he is Mark", she said. "Please buzz him. I will talk with him on the phone unless he wants to see me", I said. "Good morning Governor", I said answering the phone. "Hi Mark", the Governor said. "I know we have a meeting Thursday. Would it be possible to change the meeting to Friday afternoon or we could have two meetings?" I asked. "I will have Carol let everyone know of the change to Friday afternoon. Is there anything else", he said. "Not right now. I just have a lot of changes that need to be brought forward and I would rather not say anything until I have everything in order", I said.

"Dawn, I need Kelly Bryan now, please. If he is not in his office, I can talk with him over the phone", I said. "Hi Mark, Kelly said. "I am going to keep you busy Kelly. We have a lot to do and a short time to do it in. First, hopefully you will get new personnel next week. I need to know how my people it takes to get one apartment ready in New City and how many you have done so far." I said. We have about 15,000 in the dome and we are currently completing about 40 a day", he said. "How many buses have you been able to complete?" I said. I believe 8 as of this morning", he said. "I need you to pull half your crews and use them to help in working on the buses. I need 36 buses done priority. I need a sign to go on the buses, so get a pencil ready. Bus Lines will start in 2 weeks. Cost to ride the bus is one token. Ride buses now for FREE. Have you got the new mini generators that Sunshine was making yet" I asked? "She sent four over. She said she would have more today, but did not say how many", he said. I need you to send one of the buses over to the Tower and have them bring the keys to my office, please. Kelly, thank you for your time", I said.

"Dawn, would you please find out where I can get signs made and would you get Ms. Wells from Security on the phone if she is not in her office. Would you also inform Carol, that I need all Directors in the meeting Friday afternoon, no exceptions", I said.

"You caught me in the office? What can I do for Mr. Anglin", Mikella said as she entered the office. "Hi Mikella. We haven't met. You can call me Mark. We will need to spend a little time together over the next few weeks", I said. "Dawn, would you please bring Mikella a notebook and pen please", I said. First of all Mikella, we will put in security cameras throughout the city. I know you have four currently at each entrance and one at the Tower entrance. There is not a current problem with the cost. They will be set up every half mile along the outer and inner boardwalks. I understand it will take a while for the cameras to be hooked up and there needs to be rooms set up with multiple monitors. We will set the cameras up with a red light to show they are on. We have the time before they need to be working. I just need citizens to think they are working. We will have a lot to discuss Mikella over the next few months about a lot of changes that will happen. The cameras are a priority. Have a great day", I said. "Thank you sir", she said.

"Dawn, would you see if the Governor would have time to have lunch with me?" I asked. A few minutes past waiting for an answer. "He already has a lunch date. He said he would be happy to meet with you later if you like", she said. "Ask him when would be a good time this afternoon", I said. "About 2 PM", Dawn said. "That will work", I said. "When the young lady with the lunch cart comes by, would you let me know?" I asked. As I was flipping the switch on the telecom, I noticed the map I brought back from Waco. The map looked like someone pieced it together forming different countries within what I remember as the United States. There were fifteen states that were called the United States. Below that was one country called Reich that looked like it took in South Carolina, Georgia, Alabama and Florida. Texans took in parts of Oklahoma, Arkansas and New Mexico. On this world, things seemed to happen differently in history. Seems different areas were taken by the Germans, Russians, Mexicans, Japanese and others. I need to find me a history book, I thought. I guess I should have studied North American history in school, I thought. The lady with the lunch cart came in and I got a sandwich and some fruit.

About 1 PM a man brought me a key to the bus I ask for. I headed downstairs to take a look at it. The bus had four chairs on each side facing outward that looked comfortable. I was thinking maybe some sort of seat belt would be nice just in case. With one passenger riding next to the driver; it will hold nine total passengers. That should do nicely for now I thought. I started the bus and drove it around and back to the Tower. It handled well and was quiet. I went back up to my office. I saw Jerry come in and ask him if he would meet with the Governor and I at 2 PM. About 2 PM, the Governor got back and I asked the three Executive Assistances, our secretaries to accompany us. I wanted to get a ladies side of it. I got good feedback when they saw the bus and now for a ride. We drove south past New City. We stopped and talked to people about what they thought about the bus and having its service in the city. So far, everything seemed to be in favor of the bus. I want to start the buses tomorrow. "We will add buses as they are finished and then start charging one credit for a token. Governor, if everything goes as plan, not only will citizens be able to conveniently get around, but outsiders coming in to shop in the city will travel farther in and hopefully purchase more. I am hoping the one credit will suffice to pay for the buses", I commented. "I can see Mark where this bus will be a wonderful benefit to the community. Thank you", he said. I dropped them off at the Tower and I headed over to my tech building. Judy and Sunshine were busy working on different projects. They had gone as far as they could on the Hover Car.

I went back to the draft room and drew up plans for a four seated cart. Like a golf cart. I wanted one for me and one for the Governor and LT Governor. I figured it would take a while to get the Hover Car on line. I showed Judy and Sunshine the draft. "That was exactly what they wanted", she said. I headed over to manufacturing and showed them the draft. They said they would try to get to them as soon as they could. I had already given them enough and expected nothing right away. I went to the area where they were supposed to open the dome and allow the lumber to come in. I knew it would be a while for Jordan to get that large order of cedar coming, but I was being hopeful. I headed back to Tower. I went directly to the Governor's office. I needed to discuss with him tomorrow's meeting so he would not be caught by surprise. I let him know about the hiring of new employees, how the buses would run, and about the security cameras. I let him know that we would need additional Directors now and in the near future. He was fine with everything I told him. I left there and went over to see Marilyn. She acted as though she had not seen me in a long time. She told me how the cancer was receding and how wonderful she felt. I worked with her for about 25 minutes and then let her have her way with me. I left there and went home to rest for a while. That healing procedure takes so much out of me. It makes me feel like an old man, I thought.

I awoke to Judy shaking me. "Have I died and gone to heaven?" I said while rubbing my eyes. "No, it's just me", Judy said. "Well, you look just like an angel Judy", I said. "You did not come back by the lab and I was just checking on you", she said. "I did a healing on Mrs. Wright and I guess it took a little more out of me than I thought", I said. "I thought I would come by and see if you would like to do something tonight", she said. "Let me take a shower and I will be ready", I said. I took a quick shower and we went to dinner first at the dining facility. We then got into the bus and drove over to the Pub. There were about 50 or 60 people in the club when we arrived. "Hi Mark. What can I get you tonight?" the waitress asked. "Hi Michelle, I would like two of those very cold beers", I said. "You remembered my name. Thank you. The people here really did like your singing the last time you were here. Most did not know the songs and wondered where they were played. Some thought you might be from a different country", Michelle said. "They are mostly my songs", I said. "You won't believe how cold their beer is here Judy. I am going to come by here one day and ask them their secret. The process could be something the whole city could use", I said. We had a few beers and danced. The band asked me to sing a few songs, we danced more and we left back to my place. "It is sure nice having a ride", Judy said. "I know the walking is good for you, but it is sure nice to just sit back for a change on the way home. "Why don't you take the bus home with you", I said. "I was hoping to spend the night if you would like", she said. We then went to bed.

The next morning I took Judy to her place and I drove to the Tower. No one was there yet. I thought it would be a good time to plan out my day. I have a lot to accomplish today and I would like to leave a little early if possible. Carol was the first one in. I went out to greet her with a hug. "Could I have a few minutes?" Carol said. "I will always give you time Carol, I said. "If what I ask you is personal or confidential and you don't want to answer, that is fine. I am finding it hard to understand how someone could come in here and in three weeks be running this city. I just don't see how saving Milea would do it. As far as I know, you knew no one before you came here. I understand that you are very intelligent and a very likeable person, but not that intelligent and likeable", she said. "Carol, right now this is just between you and me. One day about a month ago, I woke up and I was not the same person. I was smarter and knew things I could never know. I even know things about another world. So overnight I was this new person. Now just that, did not get me here today. There are other people who know what and how I became what I am. I believe we are connected in ways. Some I believe are on the board of trustees. Those people are controlling me. In no way did I want to have the responsibility of running anything, especially a city and here I am now and I do it like I have been doing it all my life. I am actually a leader but don't know how I got here. Carol, I am as confused as you are. The only thing I do know and am not still sure of, because it is only a feeling is that I will only have a short time to do what I have to do and then I either die or I will be the person I used to be. Maybe I should be locked up", I said. Carol smiled and said, "I don't think you are crazy. I believe you to be a most wonderful and loving individual that really cares about people. Anyone talking to you with their eyes closed would think they were talking to a much older person. I have never been more surprised by any one individual in all my life. I guess you just need to hold on tight to the roller coaster car and see where it takes you." "I will say this Carol; you are one the most wonderful "people that I have met here in the city and the best executive assistant ever", I said. People came in so we went our separate ways.

"Good morning", Dawn said entering my office. "Please remind Director Woods that I will be at the Broadside about 10 AM. I need to find out when our signs for the buses and the bus stops will be ready. I need you to find out from Director Ryan when he feels the last bus should be finished and also the token machines for the bus stops. I will be happy to speak with them, but you can pass along the information since I will be speaking with them later today. I will be leaving a little early today. After I leave, you can also leave unless we pick up some more items that you will have to work on", I said. "Very well sir", she said. I got to the Bulkhead a little before 10 AM. The leaders had the list ready for me. "I hope you can do what you said you can do", one said. "The last of the generators will be connected today on the north side. You will not be worry about electricity loss. You were the first in the city to receive them just as I promised. After reading what you have presented, we can then negotiate terms and I will promise that we will do our best to satisfy those terms", I said. I shook hands with the Bulkhead mayor and leaders and headed back to Tower. I needed a little time to go over what the employees are wanting before the afternoon meeting.

When it came time for the meeting, I could hear everyone talking loudly of what they thought would happen, were they still going to have their jobs, were they going to have more work and most felt good things would happen. We fired no one. The meeting went smoothly. I told them about new directors and how that would reshape the city and how their current positions could change. There were considerations though on what the service employees were wanting. I gave each department jobs and things to go over before the next meeting on Tuesday. Tuesday will be a meeting to make a lot of changes to the city. Some may like them and some may not, but the changes would be good overall.

CHAPTER 12   Out Of The Pot

When the meeting finished, I went back to my place and laid down for about an hour and then took a shower and headed over to Mandy's. Mandy, Melissa, and the babies were playing close to the boardwalk. "Hi girls, are you having fun without me?" I asked. "There is no fun without you", Melissa quickly responded. "How was your day?" Mandy asked. "It is starting to get more exciting. There are a lot of things happening and a lot of new things about to happen. Have you seen any of those buses lately?" I asked. "They come by about every 30 minutes or so. They are usually full. They put a bus stop right there", Mandy said. I am hoping when all the buses run, it will make it easier for the people living here and people coming to the city to shop", I said. "Could I speak to you for a few moments?" I asked. "Sure, come on", Mandy said. "I want the three of us to go to Ktown this weekend. We could even take a little trip up to the lake", I said. "Can Melissa go to? I really don't want to leave her alone", she said. "With me, it is hard having fun with two more along", I said. "Let me think about it", she said. "I was really thinking about leaving now if possible", I said. I lightly kissed her on the lips. Mandy went over to talk with Melissa. You could see the spoiled look on Melissa's face as Mandy was talking. They talked for about 15 minutes before Mandy came back over with her pouty face. "Melissa says you don't like her. I tried to tell her you just wanted to be alone with me and Tabitha. Please reconsider Mark", Mandy said. Mandy kissed me on the face and around my ear. "Please", she said. What have I got myself into, I thought. "Okay, but I would like to leave today if that is possible," I said. When Mandy and I got to the apartment

I said, "I love you Mandy and I like spending time with you. It is hard spending real time with you when faced with the Corporation", I said. "We will do it another time", she said. I played with Tabitha while Mandy got ready. I will definitely make changes in this trip, I thought. The girls came out and we walked down the boardwalk. A bus finally came by that had 4 seats open which made the way to the entrance a lot easier.

Mandy sat in the front with me and Melissa sat in the back with the two babies. It is always nice to get out in the fresh air. That is one thing we need to fix in the city. It was dark by the time we got to Ktown. We got a two bed suite at one of the Guest Houses. I guess you can say we slept in with the babies crying at different times and going back to bed. I don't believe I am ready to be a father anytime soon, I laughed to myself because I probably have already made a bunch of women pregnant. No way out of this mess! We had breakfast in the dining room. The lady that ran the Guesthouse was real nice in helping with the babies. We left the Guesthouse and headed over to my moms. Hopefully she had no funeral or wedding going on today. My mom was out working in the nursery when we arrived. She was all smiles as usual. Her looked changed somewhat when she saw Mandy, Melissa, and the babies. "Bringing them all home to momma?" she said. I introduced everyone as we headed into the house to the living room. "The main reason I am here mom is that I want you to move to the city. You will not have to work unless you want to. You will have everything you need close by. Actually with the city, everything is kind of compact. It is nice although to get outside once in a while." "I won't know anyone there", she said. "I promise you, you will know a lot of people fast. Try it for a week and see what happens. Right now I have a two bedroom apartment right next door to mine that you can stay in", I said. "How did you manage two apartments Mark? We are only allowed one by charter", Mandy said. "Actually, right now I have eight assigned to me Mandy", I said. "What do you actually do?" my mom said. "I am executive in charge of Operations Management. It is pretty much a position of the jack of all trades", I said. "So, what do you do?" she asked again. How do you tell your mom who knows everything about you, what I do. She would never believe me if I told her what I have been doing. It is not me! There are a few me's. That even confuses me. Let's see, I am a scientist, a healer, a mechanical and electrical engineer, and entertainer and maybe even a CEO in there somewhere. It is a wonder I am still walking straight up, I thought. I just have to play the game as it unfolds. "He works for the governor", Mandy said. Now that was easy, I thought. "Let's go out to Jody's Place tonight, I said. We can find a sitter for the babies and take a night off", I suggested.

After lunch, I let the girls take the Bronco and just drive around. I stayed to be with my mom a while. "You really doing that well working for the corporation?" my mom asked. "I just happened to be at the right place at the right time and fell into a good job. I am really happy there and there are so many good people. The housing in the city is pretty compact. People there do not buy a lot of extras because there is no place to put it. People are happy though. You could cook at home or always just eat at the executive dining facility or one of the fast food places. You do not have to go far to shop and I will be right next door. You can sell or rent out the store and house", I said. "Mark, I will give it a week to see if I like it. But if I don't, you don't bother me again about it, okay?" she said. "Yes ma'am", I said. I took a few minutes and called Jordan to see how everything was going with the cedar and I called Gary to see if he was available to possibly meet us at the club tonight to take Melissa off my hands. About 7PM, we went to Barney's Steak House for dinner and then to the club by nearly 9PM. Gary was waiting outside.

"Hi Gary, I want you to meet some friends of mine. This is Mandy and this pretty young lady is Melissa. Why don't you have a beer with us?" I said. I introduced the girls to Chad, the doorman as we entered. "My sweet Loraine; have you got a table for six that you can get some cold beers to fairly quickly?" I ask the waitress. "For you honey anything", she said. She showed us a table. Gary asked Melissa right away to dance. Mandy and I got up the second dance. Bill Preston, an old family friend, asked my mom to dance. The Randy Morgan Country Band was pretty good. They have been one of the top 20 bands in this country for a while now. I saw Mandy going up and asking one of the band members something. Randy said" I have an announcement. This little gal wants me to get Mark Anglin to get up a sing her a song. I will let you use my guitar or you can use a piano if you like boy. Just get up here and sing her that song before I take her home." People started applauding. A lot of these folks knew me but did know I could sing. So I got up and went on stage like I have been doing it for years. "Now you boys probably haven't heard this song before, but if you can keep up; join right in" and I started singing "As She Is Walking Away", a Zac Brown song from one of my lives. The band did a great job of staying with me and even voiced in a few places. People were ecstatic. They were yelling, clapping, dancing and just loving the song. "I hope I did not break anyone's ears," I said as I was handing the guitar back to Randy. People were yelling more. Randy said that it looks like you got my job boy. Randy grabbed my arm and pulled me back. "One more Mark, okay?" he said. I took the guitar and mic and walked over to where my mom was sitting. "My Mom is one of the most special ladies in my life. I will sing the next one for her." I positioned the mic and sat up on the back of the chair with my feet on the seat. I sang "I Cross My Heart" by George Strait, a song from one of my lives. That song had my mom, Mandy and a bunch of other girls crying.

Then the placed roared. I took the guitar back to Randy, bowed and went to my table. People were still applauding and clapping me on the back as I walked to the table. "Well, I don't know if I can beat that", Randy said as he started playing another song. Later when the band took a break, Randy took me to the side and asked me about being a professional singer. He was telling how much they love me here. They will love me everywhere. I thanked him and told him I had other plans in mind.

As we were leaving and things were getting quiet enough to hear what someone was saying, my mother said, "when did you learn to play a guitar and sing like that?" "I don't know mom, it just happened", I said. "It seems a lot of things have been happening lately. Now I am interested more than ever to see what you do in the city", she said. Melissa left with Gary. We told her we would take care of Little Carol and see her tomorrow. We picked up the babies and went to my moms. My mom was all into taking care of those little girls. It just thrilled her to death. She never asked about Mandy and Melissa nor did she ever say anything about Judy.

The next morning, I flew out of bed scarring Mandy and the babies. "Something is wrong in the city", I said. I ran to the other room to the phone and called the Tower. The lady answering the phone said that two sheets of glass broke loose and fell in the area of the generator reservoir on the east side. One lady was in critical condition and another possibly died. I ask her to have a cart at the north entrance in about an hour I was on my way. That is the second-time structure has broken away in the last week. If there are two places, there are probably many more. I called Gary and he said he would bring Melissa right over. My mom helped Mandy get the kids ready and we were off. My mom put a sign on the door saying she needed a vacation. I guess that would work. Mr. Rice next door said he would feed and water the animals and plants.

We got to the city at 1PM. The cart was waiting for us. When we got to the site where the glass had broken lose, it was close to where Mandy and Melissa usually play. I left Mandy, Melissa, mom and the kids off and went to the hospital. The lady that was hit by the glass had the right side crushed from her waist down. "She is crushed pretty badly. I am not sure if she will make it", Doc said. The Governor came in with Dr. Williams. Dawn came up behind me. I don't know why, but I just started to cry. Dawn touched the back of my neck and rubbed, which calmed me down. "Doc, let me see if I can help her", I said. "That's a lot of pain", Doc said. I took off my shirt, and laid down next to her. She was cut up bad and still bleeding in a lot of areas. "Dawn, I will need you to place both of your hands flat on my back for as long as you can take it. You will probably pick up a lot of her pain and discomfort through me", I said. I knew Dawn had a lot of positive energy; I was just not sure what kind. Doc, I need her to stay unconscious for as long as possible. I talked to her as I was holding her in different positions. I could feel the tears coming down my face. Dawn's hands on my back felt like a brick of ice for some reason. In a way, though it soothed me. It seemed like hours had gone by when I noticed skin feeling warmer and warmer. I asked for a towel down by her private areas so I could pull her close with my hand in that position. Her toes moved. "Don't let her wake up yet Doc", I said. Dawn fell away from my back. I guess she felt the pain or was just tired out. I ran my hand up and down her body about an inch above the skin. I could feel the energy coming back. "I know this may sound weird, but I need as many people as possible to just touch me and the lady. No bad energy", I said. The ladies body tightened up then went limp. Some of the people around made noises when it happened afraid she died.

In reality, she came back. "I think she will be okay. Get her a body scan and echo to make sure, but she seems okay", I said. When I rolled over, I fell off the bed. I did not realize how small that bed was. I cried again and then passed out. When I woke up, I had a room full of people. Everybody was talking loudly. No one can ever get any sleep in a hospital", I said. I pulled myself up. Actually, I felt good. "What time is it?" I said. "You have been out for two days", my mom said. "How is the lady?" I asked. "She is doing really well. She wants to see you when you get up", Judy said with tears in her eyes. "Is Dawn okay?" I asked. "I am okay Mark", Dawn said from the corner of the room. "Well, we need to get to work. I missed a meeting already today", I said.

Sunshine stuck around and waited for me at the hospital. When I was finally ready to go, she started crying. "I was so afraid I was going to lose you Mark", she said. "You are so sweet Sunshine. I will not go easily", I said with a smile and a hug. She had a cart outside and took me over to my apartment. My mom was waiting for me. "I stayed here if that is okay", she said. "Yea mom, I will get you the key for next door if you want it. I need to change and get to work", I said. "You need to take the day off. Do you realize how many people love you Mark? I mean really love you. You will sure break a lot of hearts one day. And that girl you saved, Sheila, she thinks she will wait on you the rest of your life", she said. "I will just take it as it comes, I guess", I said. "By the way, Ralph Namor and I went out last night if that is alright?" she said. I smiled and headed over to Tower.

Everyone was so pleased to see me as though I had been gone a long time. I went directly to my office followed by Dawn. "Dawn, would you please try to find out for me who the science advisor is for the country and if I can speak with him. What I need to find out is why the domes in the cities are orange. I need to also speak with the President when he has time please", I said.

A few minutes later, Dawn had the President on the phone. "I guess you have heard about the dome? I have not inspected the welding on the dome, but I would be willing to bet we have a serious problem. I know it will cost a lot, but the dome must be rebuilt. I suggest using the new alloy for the frame and plastic instead of glass. We do not have plastic yet, but I can show manufacturing how to make nano plastic which is harder, more durable and a lot easier to handle than glass. I would need more than our manufacturing here at Capital City to complete the task. Also, it will take a lot of graphite to complete the mission. There is a layer of coal between Waco and Cameron that could be stripped mined. Graphite dust is present in layers around the coal. Then I guess you could use the coal for something else if you need it. They use it up north to heat with. Mr. President, I just don't want to see a lot of people dying if a major occurrence where to happen", I said. "I will get people working on it right away. I will get our manufacturing people over to see you. As for the land to strip mine; we may have problems with the locals", he said. "Tell them, that they will receive royalties off any coal or graphite mined", I said. "Would you have any thoughts about ending this siege at Paso City?" he said. "I believe I can make it happen, but you will have to stand behind any decision I was to make. You may not like how I handle it. I have to take care of something here in the morning, then I can head to Paso City", I said. "There will be a plane for you at the airfield", he said.

"I have a Gerald Kind on the phone for you Mark. He is one of the country's top scientists", Dawn said. "Hi Gerald, I am trying to find out what the orange color on the dome is for", I said. "People age slower under the orange dome. The women get fewer wrinkles and they love it", he said. "The problem is Gerald; it seems to cause other problems at the same time. I am sure you know of the growth caused by the generator reservoirs and I am wondering if maybe the females not having male babies may be an effect. I was thinking about alternating the dome sheets blue and orange checkerboard. The blue would allow plants to grow in the city and I believe it would be healthier overall to the citizens", I said. "That might work. It has never been tested. It would give the people more of a sense of day in the dome", he said. I was thinking also about venting out the dome, allowing fresh air in. There must be a ton of carbon dioxide in the air", I said. "I agree Mark. The President has a lot of faith in you. Keep me up to date on how everything is going", he said. "Thank you, Gerald", I said and hung up.

"Dawn, would you come in here for a few minutes?" I asked. "I need you to sit down right here", I said as I motioned her to the couch next to me. "First of all, I would really like to thank you for being there for me with that lady the other day. Did you have much pain or discomfort for the procedure?" I asked. "It started to hurt real badly, so I pulled away. I am sorry", she said. "No, no, on the contrary, you did very well thank you. When you touched me though, I was able to see two of your lives that live in you now. You're original I could not read at all. After the procedure, I am able to read people thoughts if I focus in on them, so apparently I absorbed some of your abilities", I said. "The board said you were one of the strongest Mandakes they have ever witnessed", she said. "What is a Mandake?" I asked. "Someone who collects multiple consciousness's and sometimes able to absorb another person's ability without absorbing the personality is a Mandake,' she said. One of the board members knows whenever a person becomes a Mandake. That is how we knew about you", she said. "I want to thank you again for using your energy with mine Dawn to help that girl. Tomorrow morning I will be at the Broadside at 6 AM to work with the service people, and then I will head to the airport and will be gone for a day or two. You can go with me if you like or stay", I said. "I want to go", she said. "Then I will pick you up at your apartment about 3 AM. I will have one of the buses. If you would like, you can go ahead and take off and get some rest", I said. "See you in the morning", she said. I informed Carol I would handle the meeting in the morning and then fly to Paso City and told everyone good-day and left.

Most of what the service people wanted was that they get respect. People treat them poorly. The other is the twelve hour day. I think I have the answer that will make them happy with what I have to say. I told them I would announce to the citizens of the city they will treat all people of the city as they would like themselves treated. If they did not, then they would be asked to leave the city, not to return. I made sure that it was pointed more toward the service people. I would also do checks to make sure all citizens were following this rule. I told the service people they would now have six, eight-hour shifts followed by two days off. We will close the dining facilities between 10 PM and 6 AM. All cleanups must be done during their shifts or they would go back to 12 hours. The service leaders 100% agreed to the terms. Dawn and I left and headed to the airport. She had never ridden in a Bronco before. She wanted to know why I did not get an executive car. I did not ask for one nor did they volunteer one, I told her. We got to Paso City a few hours later. Now the fun would start.

When we got to the city, I could see where a lot of the dome had come down. I was wondering how many people had died because of this. This would stop today. There must have been a thousand security guards out front behind their cars and barricades. It probably was the same on the west gate. I opened my bags and took out my weapons I made as prototypes for security for later. I ask for the person in charge. "Give me a run down. I am taking over from here", I said. He told me there were approximately two hundred and twenty men and women that took the city. They wanted higher pay and more benefits, etc. They got weapons from the security lockers. Most of the people work there, some are from other areas. They seem to have gotten the fires under control from bombs they planted, but part of the dome came down. We do not know how many citizens are dead and injured. The power is off, so they have no utilities and are probably hungry about now. We have been sending food and water in, but we know that it is not enough to feed all those people. We are basically at a loss, he told me. "Do you know or have a list of any identified terrorist in the city?" I asked. "Yes, about forty or so", he said. "I will need that now please", I said. I looked over the list of suspects. "Are any of these suspects' families living outside the city?" I asked. "About half", he said. "I want you to send teams right now to their homes and bring me all family members to the site. I need this to happen now", I repeated. "Let me know when the first family gets here", I said. About two hours past and trucks pulled up and unloading people. "Do we have an open line to the terrorist leaders?" Also do you have a connection where I can intercom to the entire city speakers?" I said. "We have both", he said.

I picked up the phone and someone came on. "Is this the leader of the terrorists?" I asked. "We are not terrorists", he replied. "Whenever a group of people take over a city and start killing people and destroying property, they are terrorists," I said. He told me his demands and I cut him off. "This stops now. I will give you fifteen minutes to answer me. I want all of you to lay down your arms and start coming out now or we are coming in. There will be no concessions", I said. "Who the hell are you", he said. "My name is Mark Anglin and I was sent here to settle this incident once and for all. The way I look at it; there are going to be a lot of citizens lives lost if something is not done. We will not give in to your demands or this could happen again in another city. It stops now", I said. "What can you do? We have these people hostage", he said. I told the security agent to open up the intercom so I can speak to the entire city. "Terrorists that have taken Paso City, listen very carefully. I am going to say this only once. If you do not lay down your weapons and come out of the city now and give yourselves up, we will come in and kill every one of you. If we have to do that, I want you to know that we will gather up all your family members, wives, husbands, children, mothers, fathers, grandpas, your dogs, and your cats if we can find them and they will all be killed. We will bury them all in a mass grave and covered in concrete. I know a lot of you came here expecting just to get some more benefits and not giving up your lives or your families lives. This incident ends now. Come out now or you will pay. We know a lot of citizens will be killed, but they will die anyway if this doesn't stop now. Some of you on the barricades look out here now and you will see dozens of your family members. We have a list of a good many of you that were already identified by monitors. If we have to shoot and kill anyone of you, your families will also be killed. It stops now", I said.

Some men and women from the barricade starting dropping their weapons and coming out. One of the terrorists shot one in the back as he was trying to leave. I fired my light gun at him burning clean through the barricade and made a two inch hole through his chest. "I just killed one of your terrorists who shot one of his own. The bad thing is now I will have to have that man's family killed when we identify him", I announced. More people dropped their weapons and coming out.

The lights were on in the Tower. With the scope on my rifle I could see figures through the window. The club tower is the only window in the tower and it is above the dome. I could see men and women and some of the figures with rifles. The phone rang. "I have the Governor, his officers and families with me. I will kill them all", he said. I focused in on one of the men with a rifle. He looked like he might be the one on the phone, but I was not sure. I fired the light gun. It took less than a second for the light to hit the glass, burn through and nearly take the arm of the terrorist. I again announced that all terrorist will leave the city now that we were coming in. If we find any with weapons, they would be killed along with their families. I told the security guards to get ready and also the guards on the west gate. As we entered the city, there were many terrorist with their hands up. We headed straight for the tower. The lights were all on here, so they managed to keep this part of the grid open somehow. Three of us got into the elevator and pushed the button for the top floor. We then climbed up into the service hatch above. When the doors opened one terrorist fired into the elevator. When he stopped, I dropped down and shot him with my light pistol. The beam hit his weapon, and then burned into his chest. The other two security guards dropped down behind me. The Terrorist dropped their weapons. I got on the intercom and notified the city that the tower was taken and that we will have all terrorists in custody soon. We will get medical help and services in as soon as possible. The Governor, his team and families were unharmed. I started thinking of how many people died during this siege. Hopefully after today, we will not see another occurrence of this. I stayed in the tower until more security guards, medical and service people came in. I then headed to the east gate. The security commander met me at the gate and thanked me. Dawn came running up giving me a hug. We headed back to the airport in one of the security vehicles. On the plane, she asked me if I would have really killed those families. I just said, I am glad I did not have to find out. Dawn could see I was down and said little on the way back to Capital City.

CHAPTER 13 Wasted Days

Over the next few days, I went nowhere. I just stayed in my apartment with a bottle of Canadian whiskey. I took the phone off the hook and did not answer the door. I had to get my head together. I could not believe I was so ruthless at Paso City. I do not want to be that type of person. I guess I put myself in a depressed state of self-pity and I had to get out of it. I finally got myself a shower, dressed and went over to the lab. Sunshine, Judy, and Rocky were busy working on whatever. I just sort of wondered in and sat at my desk. "Everyone's been worried about you", Judy said as she walked in. "It is about time you showed up for work", Rocky said. "I had a rough week", I said. "We heard what you did at Paso. You did what no one else could do", Rocky said. "Have you got anywhere with the Hover Car", I asked. "We completed everything from your specs, but we can't get it to fly", Judy said. I was remembering what Dawn said about using her ability to float and what I could remember working on them in my other life. "I want you to form a horseshoe magnet, except twist one arm upward. All positive sides down and negative sides up. When you power up the magnets, you will be sending power to both negative and positive sides at the same time. Increase the voltage until something happens", I said. I need to go up to the office and see what I missed I guess", I said. "Here is your new jolly cart", Sunshine said. It looked just like a golf cart except two seats in the back. "That is perfect Sunshine. You did a hell of a job", I said. "We all did it", she said. "Thank you guys", I said as I drove off to the tower. I parked outside the tower and went in. There were many people everywhere. I wonder what was going on. I took the elevator up to the office floor. Everyone was smiles and shook my hand and giving me hugs. "Congratulations", the Governor said and he hugged me and patted me on the back. "The Board of Directors wants to see you when you get time. Your mother has been looking for you", the Governor said. "I need to settle down first", I said as I headed for my office. Dawn followed me in.

"You okay?" Dawn asked. "Yea, I am sorry Dawn. That whole Paso deal was just more than I could handle I guess", I said. "I thought you handled it very professionally and you probably saved hundreds of lives", she said. "I know, but that just wasn't me", I said. "You have gone through a lot of changes the last few weeks. Most people would not have been able to handle it. You need to call your mother", she said. I called my mom to let her know I was all right. I ask her for dinner. She said she was having dinner with Ralph, but I could join them. I told her I would pick her up. I had to show off my new cart anyway. I went across to Ralph's office. "Question for you; I just asked my mom to dinner and she said she was having dinner with you and asked me. I want to make sure I am not intruding and I was going to bring Dawn", I said. "That will be fine Mark. We would love to have you and Dawn dine with us. Have you got a few minutes?" Ralph asked. "Yes sir, anytime", I said. "Tell me about Paso City. Are you okay?" he asked. "Ralph, I thought I commanded that situation really well. My only problem is that I don't want to be that kind of person. I told those terrorists if we had to come in, they would all die and I would kill all the members of their families. The way I looked at it, I needed to get their attention. My problem is that I would have started killing members of their families to get them out of the city. I knew most of them were talked into it not knowing what was going to happen. But it did happen and a lot of people suffered for it. We just can't let it go unpunished. I just don't want to be like that", I said with my head down. "I understand Mark. Why don't you try to take it easy for a while? You're about to burn yourself out. You have too many projects going on all at once", he said. "I will try. It just doesn't seem to happen the way I want it to. By the way, I will pick you up for dinner about 7:10 PM if that is okay", I said. I left and went back to my office. "Dawn, please have dinner with me, my mom, and the Governor this evening. By the way, have you been to the club yet?" I asked. "No, I haven't", she responded. "We are also going dancing tonight. No more calls today. I am leaving and will pick you up later", I said.

I went back to my place and laid down for a while before going next door to see my mom. We talked for a little while and we left to pick up Dawn and then to pick up the Governor. "How come I don't have one of these?" Ralph asked. "I guess I am pretty special. You will have one in a few days", I smiled. "Now this is class", he said. We had a somewhat quiet dinner with a few people coming to the table to let us know that they were there I guess. Some congratulated me. Others just were saying small talk to the Governor. After dinner, we went upstairs to the Club. I could really use a cold beer from the Pub, I thought. The waitress had a table set up for us right next to the dance floor. The orchestra really sounded great. Then they asked me to sing. I don't know why, but it completely slipped my mind they would ask me. The song that came to mind was a Josh Groban song from one of my lives. That was something maybe I needed to hear myself. The song is "You Raise Me Up." That song always gave me chills and made me feel really, good. I played a little on the piano to show the orchestra the song. That way whoever could key in would have a better idea of the song itself. I started playing then singing. Some people danced and then stopped and just listened. About half way through, I could hear my voice rattling and I know I had tears in my eyes. After the song, people kept applauding me as I walked across the floor to the table.

"That was beautiful", my mom said. Dawn took my hand and squeezed it. I felt like I was about to cry thinking about Paso City. I gained my composure back and ask my mom to dance. I then dance with Dawn a few dances. I don't know which life it was from, but my dancing became really good. About as good as Fred Astaire, I thought. People were watching the moves as Dawn and I went around the floor. They were applauding as I made some marvelous moves. Dawn stayed right with me like we had been dancing with each other for years. "Is there anything you don't do?" Ralph asked. "I don't know Ralph, it seems every time I need to do something, the old brain starts kicking out instructions. I don't know where it comes from", I said. The band asked me to sing another song. I sang "My Heart Will Go On" and then "Don't Cry for Me Capital City." I then sat down for another drink. We sat there for another hour talking small talk, dancing and I sang one more song and we left. I took Ralph home, then Dawn and my mom and I went home.

"I want to speak with you Mark", my mom said. I opened her door and we sat down on the couch. "I am not sure if I know you anymore. You have changed a great deal over the last month Mark. What has been going on?" she asked. "It is really hard to explain. You will have a hard time believing what I am going to say, but try to stay with me", I said. I started with the day I woke up feeling different and how everything changed as the days passed until now. I told her I feel like I am still changing, growing in some way. She just sat there for a little while, not saying anything with this astonished look on her face. "Mom, there are a lot of good things that are happening because of what is happening to me. I am helping a lot of people and that is why I think this is all happening to me. I just have to wait to see how it all ends," I said. She said that no matter what happens, she will be there for me. We hugged and I kissed her and said goodnight. I went back to my apartment.

When I opened the door to my apartment, Judy was sitting on the couch. I guess I had better lock my door, I thought. What if I brought someone home with me? "Hey there", she said. "Hi Judy. Have you been waiting long?" I asked. "About an hour. Are you off for the weekend?" she asked. I did not even know what day it was. "What day is it?" I asked. "Friday, come sit", she said. She put her head on my shoulder. "What can I do to get you feeling better? I know you had a very hard week. Everyone was knocking on your door and you would not come out. There was even talk about kicking your door in", she said. "I am sorry; I guess I was just feeling sorry for myself. I did not like the person I was becoming. The Paso City incident nearly killed me inside", I said. We just sat there for quite a while, then got up and went to bed. I made sure I locked the door first.

I did not hear my alarm go off. I guess Judy turned it off. I smelt food cooking. I got up and Judy had breakfast about ready. I think she just about cooked everything. "I was not sure what you wanted, so eat what you want", she said with a smile. "Mandy has been calling asking about you the last few days", she said. "I guess I need to call her and let her know everything is okay", I said. "You love her", she said. "Yes, my problem is, I love both of you very much and feel I can't do anything about it. She is like the mom type and you are like the model type, I guess which makes you more exciting. I have so much to accomplish and I feel like I need to do these things before I can do anything for myself. I know that leaves you on the sideline waiting and you will only wait so long. I don't know what to do. I just know I am tired", I said. She came up behind me and kissed me on the back on the head and rubbed my shoulders. "I will tell you this Mark. I have never met a man so intelligent, sensitive and yet can dance and sing. You have all the qualities anyone could ask for. I will do my best to be here for you even if I am second in line", she said. "You will always be my angel", I said.

"I want to show you something today Judy. Let's go for a ride in my new cart", I said. We rode over to manufacturing then out past where the new deck was being built, out through the opening. On the other side was a pretty pond surrounded by Desert Willows and Oak trees. There was a cool breeze blowing across the pond. It was about 100 degrees, but it felt good outside. I brought a blanket I threw across the grass by the water. We just laid there for hours not saying much. It was just a nice peaceful day and talking may have even messed it up, I thought. It was about 2PM and the sun shifted again where we were out of the shade. We packed up and went back inside. "Would you like to go to the dining facility or to a fast food somewhere", I said. "Let's just drive and when we see something we like, we can stop", she said. We headed south down the boardwalk. We were getting close to the south entrance when Judy said to stop. "Grandmas Home Cooking, she said as she read the sign. Just what the doctor ordered." They had the best chicken fried steak ever. I had better not tell Big Mike, I smiled to myself. We left there and headed back home. I took Judy home and then went back to my place. My mom was sitting outside just taking in everything. I sat down next to her. "Have a good day", she asked. "I was out with Judy", I said. "How many girlfriends do you have?" she asked. "I love them all", I said. She just smiled. "Are you and Ralph going out again tonight?" I asked. "He hasn't called yet. I hope so", she said. I won't get in your way this time", I said. "You are never in the way", she said. "I need to call Mandy", I said. I got up and went inside.

I called Mandy and set a time to come over. I made sure I locked my door. This is crazy, I smiled to myself. When I got to Mandy's, Melissa and Gary were outside playing with Little Carol. "Did you decide to move to the city Gary?" I said. "Yea, I got a job here right away", he said. "Are we going out tonight?" Melissa said. "I guess so", I said reluctantly. "I like your ride", Gary said. "Yea, they made it just for me and two friends", I said. We dropped the kids off at the Children's Center and headed to a fast food place. We left there and went to the Pub. I don't know why, but I just like this place. It reminds me of Jody's back home. When we walked in Michelle came running up. "I just wanted to make sure I got you for a customer before one of the other girls got you", she said. "Got the weekends now I see Michelle', I said. "Yes, one of the girls got married and did not think she needed to work anymore. I am so excited you are here. I hope you sing us one of you new songs again", she said. Michelle brought us four beers. "Damn, these beers are cold", said Gary. The band was country. We will be two-stepping tonight. We danced and I sang songs with the band. I even sang one of the songs they knew. We left before closing and headed back. I really was tired and I had the feeling Mandy was not going to let me rest. I spent the night with Mandy and headed back home in the morning. Driving back my mind rattled again. These last days have been wasted. I have accomplished nothing at all.

Just as I was about to open my door, my mom stuck her head outside of hers telling me that Dawn came by. I went in a sat on the couch and put my feet on the table. I closed my eyes. The phone rang and I woke up. I don't know how long I slept. It was Dawn. She wanted to know why I did not call her yesterday. I told her I did not know that I needed to. "Mark, I just wanted you to know that I had the best time of my life Friday night. I have never been with anyone like you before. I would love to do it again if you want", she said. "We will see Dawn. I will see you in the morning", I said. I went to bed. This would be a rough week again. I thought about my mom. She did not ask me to take her home. Maybe she liked Ralph enough to stay, I thought.

The alarm went off and I was up and out. No one tried to wake me. At least I did not hear them if they did. I got plenty of rest and was ready to get back to work. I did not seem to do much last week. I got in my cart and drove to the Tower. There were two other carts parked there. I guess they delivered Ralph's and Jerry's carts. That should please them. I went to the office. Carol and Dawn were at their desk. Sunshine popped up out of nowhere with all smiles as usual and came running to give me a hug like a 16 year old. She sure can make your day. "I brought the boss's mini cars", she said. "Sunshine, I want you to do me a favor. I want you to build me a cart and paint it pink. I want you to put a smiley sun on the front and sides of the car in yellow and paint the word Sunshine on the car somewhere. Would you do that for me?" I asked. I thought she would scratch her head for a moment. She smiled and said, "you got it boss." Carol could not stop laughing.

"Here is your pay stubs the last weeks. I think you only got the first one", Carol said. I really have not been interested in how much I made. I just want to do what I came here for", I said. I thanked her for the stubs and went to the office. Dawn followed me in. "Sit Dawn", I said as I walked over to the couch. "I want to thank you for the wonderful time on Friday, but that was not a date. I just thought we both needed to take a break. I am sorry if I made you feel anything different. I can't date my assistant", I said. "You date Judy and she is your assistant in the lab", she said. "That is sort of different. I dated her before I ask her to work with me. She has an electrical engineering background I needed for my projects", I said. "Well then, if the only way that I will be able to go out with you again is quit; then I quit", she said. "What are you going to do?" I asked. I will become one of those directors you need to hire. I am smart enough", she said. "Where will I find an assistant as good as you", I said. "That is your problem. Now try to get rid of me", she said as she walked out of the office. Carol called me on the intercom. "What's going on?" she said. "I think I made Dawn upset", I said. I sat back at my desk and opened up the pay stub from last Friday. I guess my curiosity got the best of me. I had over five million credits on my account. Why are they still paying me all this money? I asked myself.

Mr. Rice from Antonio Manufacturing called to let me know that the framing I requested was on schedule and the first twenty loads would be delivered Wednesday. He told me that Paso City got the first loads to repair their dome. He also told me they got the order on how to make my nano plastic. He said that they hoped they had it right. The first sheets should be ready by this weekend. I called John Ryan and ask him to have two foot diameter poles 40 foot long; twenty foot high and twenty foot deep. I knew we had a large supply of forty footers to the east of the city. As soon as the poles are in place I would like to have the dome broken down over New City first. I told him the framing would come in on Wednesday. He told me he had a feeling we would start working on the dome after that little girl's death and the breaking over Broadside. He was prepared to have at least three thousand personnel start on the dome. He knew this would be a priority and had to be done hopefully before we got any bad weather.

I walked over to Carol's desk. "What did you say to make her mad?" she said. "I made the mistake of taking her to dinner and dancing Friday night. Now I guess she thinks we are inseparable. I sure do have a lot of women problems", I said. "You need to slow it down", Carol smiled. "I never thought I was that good looking", I said. "It's your charm", Carol said. "Is the Governor in yet?" I asked. "He just came in. Go on in", she said. "Good morning Ralph", I said as I entered the office. "Did Carol give you the keys to your new buggy that was parked at the

Tower entrance?" I said. "No, but I wondered who they belonged to", he said. "One for you and one for Jerry", I said. "Sit, I thought I told you to take some time off", he said. "We need to get to work on the dome. The first shipments of framing will be here on Wednesday and the first shipments of plastic to replace the glass by the weekend. Antonio Manufacturing is doing a splendid job of getting the job done. John Ryan said he would start today placing the new support poles in. I am having the city expanded by six hundred yards all around. Instead of the dome circling to the ground, it will stop at the new support poles and a wall will be built. That will allow us greater access to bring supplies in or for expansions later on", I said. "I would not have been able to do what you have done Mark. You have done such an excellent job here. I am afraid that the board might try to take you away from me", he said. "I am not going anywhere, at least for a while", I said. "You do whatever you need. You will have my support and the support of the Corporation", he said. "By the way; we are bringing in a lot of new people, most of which are men. In a few weeks, I would like to throw a big party, invite a few big popular bands and see if we can get some of these new people to meet our citizens and invite them properly", I said. "That is a great idea. Take whoever you need for help and make it happen", he said. I left and headed back to my office. "I have a new assistant coming over today. Let's see if you can hold on to this one", she said smiling. "One day I am going to take you away from Ralph", I said.

I just sat down at my desk and Judy called. "Please come down to the lab right now Mark. You have got to see this", she said. I told Carol where I was going and headed to the lab. Everyone was laughing and playing with the large disk that was the prototype for the Hover Car. It was about a foot off the ground and they had it going all over the place. "You did it," I yelled. We just hugged each other and laughing. "Where is the champagne?" Judy said. "We have to get the car going first", I said. Sunshine sat down on it and it dropped a bit but held her weight. It nearly threw her off though. "Now we have to perfect it. The magnets may also need to be adjusted like on the generator. We will just have to play with it and see. I noticed how friendly Rocky and Sunshine were. Good, I hope they get together, I thought.

I took off my jacket and tie and starting looking the disk over. We opened up the base plate and started playing with the magnets to see if adjusting them helped with the conversion of gravity. Sunshine said it would make it a lot easier to put magnets on the floor. I said that would be fine until you go a foot or so off the ground. Sunshine said she would be okay if the cars stayed close to the deck. We played with it for nearly two hours. Rocky had an idea of running two currents at the same time from different directions. We tried it with two small generators. The disk hummed. It was running now. We put the plate back on and Rocky sat on the disk. We started it and it floated up about four and half to five feet. "It works", he said. "Now we just need to equip it with four seats like the carts and put seatbelts on the seats and we will see how it holds up. "I have all the parts", Sunshine said. Between the four of us in each other's way, we finished the car in about three hours. All four of us got on the car and we moved around the room. The car held up nicely. Now we need to attempt it outside at greater heights to see how everything will work. I took the car up first by myself. I flew up over the buildings first making sudden moves to see if it would handle well. I then flew all the way up nearly to the top of the tower. After landing, Rocky said he wanted to drive. We all got on and Rocky took us for a ride of our lives. Judy was nearly screaming in fear from some of the sharp turns he made. People came outside to look up at us. This was great, I thought. We landed the car next to the tower and Sunshine went up to the executive offices to tell them to come and see. It was not long and hundreds of people were standing around waiting for us to take off. I asked the governor if he would like to ride and he volunteered. I stayed on the ground with Judy and the governor, another executive, Sunshine and Rocky took off. Maybe I should have let Sunshine drive, I thought. Rocky took it easy on them though. He went to the top of the dome, flew over New City and back. When they landed the governor said, "the President is going to want to see this." When the governor stepped off, he was a little rocky. It was like having sea legs. He shook our hands and went up to Tower to report. "We need to create some ambulances for the hospital now", I said as we flew back to the lab. I told everyone that we should go to the Pub tonight and I did not care if they were late in the morning.

CHAPTER 14 I Want Coffee

After we left the club, I took everyone home and I stayed with Judy that night. She is always a remarkable woman. She never complains and is always there for me. I guess Mandy is to, just in a different way. I left Judy's early and went to the lab. I had a dream about cappuccino coffee. I was wondering if I could make a cappuccino machine. I used to love cappuccino in one of my lives. I sat down at the draft table and drew. Sunshine and Rocky came in about 10 AM. "Look here. Do you think we could throw one of these together?" I asked. "What is it?" Sunshine and Rocky said at once. "It is a cappuccino coffee machine. You would love the coffee Sunshine", I said. They took the draft over to a corner and went over it. I told them I needed to check in at the office. I started to take the Hover Car but took the cart instead. When I got up to the office, people were talking about the Hover Car. I guess I should have brought it with me. "The President loved the idea of your new Hover Car. He wants one delivered to Antonio as soon as you can get another made", Carol said. "You're going to love your new assistant. She is gorgeous", Judy said. "That is all I need", I said as I walked over to her desk. "I am Courtney Mr. Anglin", she said holding her hand out. I shook her hand and ask her to follow me. "Sit. I need someone who is going to get things done when I ask. You may have to travel with me. If you do not know something, please don't waste time looking for the answer, ask and save time", I said. I was trying to be rough. She just smiled and said yes sir. "Please call me Mark. Also, if I were to give you a hug, it does not mean I want you. It means I am happy or maybe I just need a hug", I smiled and said. "Dawn was pretty organized. She left a list of names and phone numbers on the desk. I will be having you call most of them a lot", I said. I told her she could go to her desk.

Ralph called on the intercom. "Do you want me to split the bonus fee for that new car to your associates at the lab?" he asked. "If you would Ralph, I would appreciate it. I think I am rich enough", I said. "Okay, I will let Carol know", he said and hung up. "Courtney, see if you can get someone over at the Antonio Manufacturing plant for me", I said over the intercom. A few minutes had passed and the phone rings. "Hi Mark, this is George over at Antonio Manufacturing. What can I do for you?" he asked. "You all are making those sheets of plastic for the dome. I was wondering if it would be possible to have plastic cups made. Not cups with a handle. Just plain plastic cups with a little lip on them to support a cap that might snap on. Would you be able to do something like that?" I asked. "Well Mark, we make cups, we will just change a few things around and see what we come up with. The President has already given orders to give you whatever you ask for", he said. "Well, thank the President for me. Have a great day George" and I hung up.

I had lunch with Ralph, my mom, Jerry and Marilyn at the executive dining and went over some of the things that would happen over the next week. I then went back over to the lab. Sunshine and Rocky were playing with the Hover Car. Judy went over to manufacturing to discuss details with them. I told them they could expect a bonus in the next Friday pay day. Sunshine was running around saying she would be a millionaire. I told them to finish up whatever they were on and take the rest of the day off if they wanted. I called Judy over at manufacturing and told her the same. I went back to my place. I don't know why, but I just seem tired a lot. I have been getting enough sleep and I don't feel sick. I laid down and took a nap. I awakened to Dawn tugging on my arm. I guess I forgot to lock the door again. "What's up?" I said. "Is that new girl as good as I am?" she asked. "I don't know Dawn, I was not in the office long enough to talk with her or find out what she did or did not know", I said. "Well, you should not have let me go", she said. "I did not let you go. You left", I said. "Humph", she made a noise while sitting down next to me. "So what are we going to do?" she said. "I don't know Dawn. You just woke me up", I said. We did not say anything for a while. "What is with all the jealousy and tantrums Dawn?" I asked. "I am just upset", she said. "Tell me why", I said. "You don't understand. I had a really wonderful time the other night. I mean it was like no other night I have ever had. You were such a wonderful date. I thought you liked me more than you have shown today", she said. "As for liking you Dawn; I think you are awesome. You're beautiful, smart, sweet and a great dancer. As for a date; maybe I should have clarified that. I took you out to just get out and do something. You were there with me. I just did not put anymore into it because you work with me", I said. "Well, I don't work with you anymore. What do you want to do?" she asked. She took her blouse off and then her slacks. She had a perfect body. She then let her dark black hair down which came down to her lower back. She was perfect. My mind clicked. She looked like a younger version of Sarah. Again I was in awe. I couldn't help from asking; "do you have a sister named Felicia?" She came over and sat next to me in her bra and panties. "How do you know my sister", she asked. "She is Milea's best friend and a friend of mine. I did not connect you two until I saw you with your hair down and your perfect figure. You look just like your mom. I have also met your brothers", I said. "Is there anyone you don't know Mark?" she asked. "She never mentioned you when I last spoke with her", I said. "That is a long story. I haven't spoken with her in about seven years. "My father was trying to have his way with me back when I was a teenager. My mom would not believe it when I told her. He tried to get his way with me for about a year until I turned eighteen and left home. Soon after, I had that entity come into my head and I worked for Corporate. I guess she finally found out about him and divorced him", she said. "I don't know Dawn, she never mentioned him, nor did Felicia. You should talk to Felicia. She really is a sweet young lady", I said. "Actually, I would love to", Dawn said as she started crying. I hate it when things get all emotional now. One person inside of me must have been really emotional, I thought. Tears came from my eyes. I was doing my best to keep my composure and hold Dawn. I really did feel bad for her now. She finally fell asleep on my shoulder. I picked her up and laid her on the bed and closed the door. I went back to the living room and picked up my drafting pad and began to sketch. My crazy head started clicking again. Now that I knew how the antigravity unit works, I planned some off beats. I thought about what would happen if Texans ever were attacked. There was only a small guard and security force untrained for combat. With the light guns I created, I believe I can make some strong weapons.

I went next door to speak to my mom. I needed to find out if she was going home Saturday or Sunday. She said she needed to go by Sunday. That she was planning on selling everything and moving to the city. You never know when selling property. Sometimes you get a buyer right away. She said her and Ralph were going to dinner and if I wanted to come. I told her I would pass.

I had to do something about Dawn. I was not sure how to handle her. I really liked her, but I did not need another romance going right now. I needed to do something about Mandy. After the last weekend, I lost interest in her. She seemed to always have something in the middle of us, especially

Melissa. I want no one mad at me, but my personal problems seem to hinder things I came here to accomplish. I don't even know what I came here to accomplish, I thought. Well, I can't leave Dawn in my bedroom. I shook her arm trying to wake her without getting too close. She grabbed my arm and pulled me toward her. "Come here. Hold me", she sleepily said. I laid down next to her and she snuggled up to me. We fell asleep for about an hour when I felt her struggling to remove my clothes. She had already taken her underwear off. She had perfect 38 breasts with large nipples. I helped her take off my clothes. We made love for about an hour then showered without saying much. We then went to one of those fast food places that served a Tex-Mex. At least I called that it. We then went up to the club and danced until midnight. I sang a few songs that the orchestra asked me to sing. I then took Dawn home telling her I had to get up early and go outside the city in the morning. I went home and locked the door.

My mom came over the next morning asking me to go to Ktown this afternoon. I told her I would. I could come back Sunday evening or Monday morning, I thought. I went over to the lab to hang out just in case Dawn showed up. Judy was busy working on the cappuccino machine. "I thought Sunshine was going to do that", I said. "I did not have anything to do so I came in. This machine was staring me in the face. I was wondering how this machine was going to match up to the others you came up with Mark", she said. "It will be one of the best inventions ever. Wait till you taste the coffee that comes from it", I said. "I don't know where you get all these ideas", she said. We worked on the machine for two hours and finally got the coils in place and plugged it in. This machine would be a smaller version of the one I have in mind. This one should make about thirty cups, the large one should make at least a hundred; at least I hope it would, I thought. Judy went over to the market and got milk while I loaded the coffee, sugar, and water. I am hoping the milk exchange worked properly to foam the milk. I mixed enough to make about ten cups to start off with. Judy came in with the milk. I mixed about a 3rd coffee and milk, then foamed about 3rd milk and added sugar. I put the cup under and presto! It came foaming out like it is supposed to. I tasted it first. Maybe a little too much sugar I thought. Judy put her cup under the spout. "This is pretty cool", she said. She tasted it. "This is the best coffee I have ever tasted. It is sort of like drinking cocoa. Now what are we going to do with it?" she said. "We are going to sell it. Well, maybe not us, but I plan on getting someone to open a cappuccino shop and sell nothing but donuts and cappuccino and maybe regular coffee. They could have carts deliver to the different offices in the morning. Open maybe from 6 AM until maybe noon every day. What do you think?" I said. "I don't know. Most offices have coffee machines. I guess you can try it and see what happens", she said. "Monday I will take some coffee up to the office and see what the ladies say. Then we can go from there", I said. "What's on for this evening?" she said. "I am going to take my mom home", I said. "Just wondering if you were in the mood for dancing," she said. "Pack a bag and go with us to Ktown", I said. "It will take me ten minutes", she said. I drove her over to her place then back to mine. I packed a bag then checked on my mom. We waited for about twenty minutes on her and we headed for the north gate. As we were driving to Ktown, my mom said, "why don't you buy a new car? Ralph said you could more than afford it", she said. "I just haven't made the time yet and it really has not been that important to me. I will tell you what; if we get back in time, I will go to Jed's and get a new car", I said. Judy and my mom got along real well together. They seemed to always have a connection with whatever the subject was.

I dropped them off at the house and I drove over to Jed's. "Hey Mark. You ready to trade that old Bronco in for a real vehicle", he said. "What is the best looking vehicle you have on the lot? I don't care what the price is. I need it today if possible", I said. "I have the new Mark I, but it might be a little more than you may think", he said. "Let's take a look", I said. "It's a four door luxury pickup. It has all the bells and whistles you will find in any expensive vehicle", he said. "Can you take credits Jed or do I need to take a quick trip to the bank?" I said. I can take the credits. You understand the exchange rate is different in dollars?" he said. "I understand." I looked at the maroon Mark I. It was actually really a beautiful truck. I could never have dreamed owning anything like this in my life. The 23 year old was showing in me, I thought. Jed ran the credits on his machine. He looked up with a surprised face and said", it says you are good to go Mark." Jed has known my family all his life and he knows we have never had the money to buy anything like this before. He sort of scratched his head for a moment and asked. "What about the Bronco?" he asked. "I don't care Jed. Do what you want with it. This is all I need", I said as I walked out of his office tossing the keys in the air up and down. I then drove home. I did not mention the truck and I guess they figured I did not get a new car because they did not ask.

Judy and my mom were in the kitchen talking and laughing about something as I picked up my drafting pad and walked outside. My mind clicked again. Before I died in one of my lives, I was working on a light cannon for a satellite. I remember on a full spread beam it could wipe out a large part of a city. I know I could not do that without being far out. I could see how to build it piece by piece in my mind. I drew it out on paper. Judy came out and sat down next to me. "What are you working on?" she said. "It is another weapon", I said. "What do we need another weapon for?" she said. "I haven't decided yet to build it, but if I do, it will have to be secret even from the Corporation", I said. "I won't dig anymore", she said. We just sat there, not doing much of anything. "Let's go dancing tonight", I said. "Dancing sounds good to me Mark. Your mom was talking about going to Jody's earlier", Judy said. "We could get some barbecue and then head over there", I said. We laid down for a while before going out. My mom had said she was tired to. Mom woke us up about 7PM. Judy fixed herself up. I just put on a cap and we headed out the door to Barney's Steak House for barbeque. "Mark", my mom nearly yelled. It is beautiful", she said. "Yea and the name of the truck is Mark. Here look", I said as I showed her the trade name on the side of the truck. As we got in Judy said how beautiful it looked and how comfortable it was. We arrived at Jody's about 9PM. That was usually when the band started anyway. The Randy Morgan Band was playing. I need to speak to him about Capital City. Randy saw us as we came in and waved. The place wasn't filled yet and we had a choice of tables.

I ordered beers and Judy grabbed my hand to dance. "I have been trying to learn country dance and still have not got it down right", Judy said. "All you need to know is to follow my lead Judy", I said. After a few songs, Randy came to the table. "Hey Mark, how are you doing. I was wondering if you would sing that song you sang last time you were here. The song "As She Was Walking Away" was a big hit. I would also love to learn it if you don't mind", he said. "No problem", I said. "Do you sing at all the clubs?" Judy asked. I began to sing and people stopped dancing and clapped to the beat of the song. When I finished, everyone wanted more. I sang a couple more songs and sat down. Randy took a break and came over to the table. When you get a chance, would you write down some of those songs?" he asked. "I will make a trade Randy. If you will agree to come to Capital City for big splash, I will have hopefully next month; I will give you all the songs you want. I will also pay you", I said.

"If you promise to get on stage and sing with the band, I will promise we will be there", he said. We sat and drink a beer together and he got up and went back to the band. Mom found a partner to dance with and Judy and I ripped up the floor. It was getting close to midnight and my mom was getting tired. Randy asked me to sing one more. He wanted to hear that song I sang to my mom last time. I looked around the room and found a young lady sitting with some friends. She did not seem to have a date, so I took one of the bands guitars and went over to their table and sat in front of her. When I finished the song, she was smiling, laughing and crying all at the same time. I made someone's evening, I thought as I walked away smiling.

When I sat down Judy said that what I did was really nice. My mom gave me a hug. As we were about to leave, the young lady ran up and gave me a hug and thanked me. That made my evening. It did not take long to get home. Mom took a bath and went straight to bed. Judy and I sat up and talked for a while. I told her there would be some big changes coming up in this state. This is why I was sent to the city. I will get with Sunshine and Rocky when we get back. I need to find about another half dozen people I can trust that can keep a secret no matter what. I then told Judy what I thought would happen. I don't know how I know; I just know it will happen. I told her I thought there would be a war in the coming months. It could be six months or could be a year, but probably before a year. I knew what I was telling her would scare her, but she will get scared sooner or later and I needed to know that she would be with me all the way.

The next morning I got up about 7:30 AM. I got in my truck and went over to a friend of mine. He worked as a welder and knows how to put just about anything together. I woke him up. His girlfriend was not too happy with me. "Sorry to wake you on a Sunday Tommy, but I need to speak with you", I said. "Anytime Mark. We have been best friends all our lives", he said. "I need you to bear with me a moment and let me give you some background of what I am doing, or at least some of what I have done", I said. I filled him in of some of the things I have accomplished over the past month. He found most hard to believe since he has known me most of my life. "Let me ask you something. If a man three hundred pounds were to haul off and hit you knocking you about ten feet; what would you do?" "I would find a two by four and cut him down to size", he said. "That is what I am looking for; people who can use their heads. If you would have said fist to fist, I would worry about you. How much are you making now?" I asked. "About five thousand a month", he said. "What if I could pay you 8,000 credits and at the end of the total assignment whether two months or twelve months, I will pay you 100,000 credits, would that interest you?" I said. "If you can find two other people like you, I will pay them 7,000 credits and the same bonus at the end of the assignment", I said.

"Is Gary Night still around Tommy?" I asked. "Yea, he moved over close to Tembel. I know how to get a hold of him though", he said. "Is he still building those remote airplanes?" I asked. "He built an airstrip out by the lake to fly those things. Some of them are pretty cool", he said. "Let me get his number from you please", he said. He wrote the number down on a piece of paper. "Can you start work this week Tommy?" I asked. "I might be able to wrap things up by Thursday", he said. "When you get to Capital City, go to the Human Resources at the Tower. Tell them you work for me. They will tell you how to find me", I said. I left there and headed home. Judy and my mom were sitting at the table drinking coffee. "Where have you been?" my mom said. "I have been out recruiting. I need more people for a project I am getting ready to start", I said. "Judy, if I can get a hold of this guy, do you want to take a ride over to Tembel?" I asked. I went to the phone and called the number Tommy gave me. A lady answered the phone and told me Gary was out at the lake. She gave me directions and Judy and I headed over there. There were about a dozen people out there flying their planes. Some saw my new pickup and came over to look. "Hi Gary", I said. "The ladies' man. What's up Mark? You have never been out here before", he said. "I am looking to hire people who can build and fly those planes. I would also need those people to train others to fly", I said. Anyone that knows how to build those remote units will be paid 8,000 credits a month. All those that know just how to fly will get 6,000 credits a month and all of those can build the remote systems will also receive a one 100,000 credits bonus at the end of the assignment. The assignment could be from six to twelve months. I am not sure yet", I said. "If you have the materials and a place to work, I can make it happen", he said. "I can take you as early as next week. Just report to Human Resources and tell them you work for me and they will point you the way", I said. "These guys are going to be happy they can get paid to fly", he said. One of the guys listening in said he would be there. Judy and I left there and went over by the lake. I had brought a blanket to spread out. We just laid there talking for about an hour enjoying the breeze and the water.

We left the lake and headed over to Jordan's house. He was outside piddling in the yard. "Nice truck. You're going to ask the impossible again, aren't you?" he said. "Probably, I need enough lumber to build a 50,000 square foot warehouse. I need it yesterday as usual. I want the floor and the ceiling joists of two by tens. The floor joists can be made of pine instead of cedar. The rest of the framing will be out of cedar as usual. I need three-quarter pressed ply-board for the roofing. I will pay for whatever overtime is needed to get the job done. Work them

Saturday and Sunday. I don't want the guys working though where they will be too tired and cause safety issues. I will get a hold of the bank and have a two hundred and fifty thousand deposit sometime Monday to get started. You can get paid from the bank like last time Jordan", I said. "You know, you are hiring up all the good help around here don't you. That leaves little for me to pick from Mark", he said. "Sorry Jordan, I have been picking up most of my people from Boone and Dal cities. I will need more as soon as I can build apartments, so when you finish this project, you can mill more wood as fast as your men can do it", I said. "Does this mean I get no more weekends off?" he said. "That is up to you Jordan", I said. "Boone city called and wanted to place a large order and I had to turn them down. I found them a small mill closer to them. I am hoping they can hire enough people to get it done", he said. Judy and I left and went back home. Mom had lunch going when we came in. It sure smelled good.

Mom said she called someone to list the property. Our neighbor said he would take the animals since he was taking care of them all ready. Mom said she would stay and close everything out. She said she would drive to Capital City when everything was done. Judy and I headed back to Capital City about 4 PM that afternoon. I was thinking about parking my new truck out here. No one steals anything, but I guess I was worried about damage. Security held my cart for me, so we did not have to wait for a ride. I took Judy home and told her I was going to the lab. When I opened the door to the lab, there were like fifty boxes stacked to one corner. I saw one box had been opened. It was the cups I ordered. Damn, they must have worked overtime to do them. I will call them in the morning and thank them, I thought. I went to the draft room and wrote things to do list for Monday. It would be a full day and I did not want to forget anything. About 7:30 PM Judy called and asked if I was interested in dinner. We went to the executive dining facility. It seemed like everyone was dining about the same time. The Governor, LT Governor, all the directors and the corporate executives either waved or said hi as we entered. After dinner, we went up to the club for a beer. We left there about 9 PM and went to Judy's.

I got up at 6 AM and went home leaving Judy sleeping. I showered and put on a suit. I headed over to the lab. I put on my coveralls and made cappuccino. Sunshine had welded me a cart and painted it. It looked good for a quick job. I pushed it over to the Tower. When I got to the office, many people were already there and coming in. I gave out cups of cappuccino. No one had ever tasted anything like it. It made a hit. I asked them how they felt if someone came every morning with cappuccino and warm donuts. Carol said she would hate me because she would gain too much weight. I had an office boy take the cart back over to the lab for me. I took off my coveralls and sat at my desk. I asked Courtney into the office.

I gave Courtney a list of people that needed to be called throughout the day starting with the President. I gave her a list of assignments to type up for me and errands to run. Courtney was really a polite young lady and ready to take any order I asked her. "The President is on the line", she said. "Mr. President, how are you today?" I said. "Doing well Mark, what can I do for you?" he asked. "You know I come up with things when it seems we will need them. First item though is just intuition. I feel we are going to have a very big problem from another country. I do not know what the board is doing, but apparently it is making someone very nervous. Your board has the ability to read minds or at least sense something going on. I believe we have spies in our cities from another country. We somehow need to dig them out and get rid of them", I said. "One of the board members also said the same thing Mark. We have people in different cities with the ability to read minds and now that they know about the spies, we will hopefully be able to detect them", he said. "That sure makes me feel a lot better Mr. President", I said. "Now because of the larger problem of a threat from another country; I need to let you know that I am working on a project that will be kept secret from everyone, even the board until it is needed. I do not want anyone coming to check up on me or my people. I hope you understand why I am doing this", I said. "I understand completely Mark and I will abide by your wishes. You will have anything you need to complete any project you are working on", he said. "I would appreciate that", I said. "Now to let you in on some information that is confidential, but probably causing the worry you have. The Corporation is trying to obtain all the territories north of Texans to Canada which includes the Dakota Territories. That would split this continent in half. That is worrying some of the other countries", he said. "I guess it would. That would give the Corporation a lot of power plus the natural resources. I know you may not know it, but the Dakotas have enough oil to supply this whole continent for the next thousand years. I could show you areas of high gold, silver, coal and graphite when we get time", I said. "That is why we depend so much on you Mark. I will be getting back to you in a couple of days. I have a meeting right now", he said.

"Mr. Ryan is on the phone", Courtney said. "Hi John, I know you don't like hearing from me", I said. He laughed and said, "Mark you can have anything you want." "John, I know you have a lot of irons in the fire. I am trying to get you more workers. We will probably need to build more homes for them. Besides the dome being a priority, I need a fifty thousand foot warehouse built north of the manufacturing deck. It needs outside access to the dome. And, of course, I need it yesterday.

Lumber will be coming next week. Part of the lumber will be pine. That will be used for the floor and roof joists only. I am sorry to put more on you, but that is a Corporate priority", I said. "I will send a team over there today and start clearing off the area for you", he said. "I appreciate your time John and by the way John, if you ever need a personal favor, please do not hesitate to call. I will do my best to fulfill it", I said.

I called Courtney on the intercom to call the next person. "Mikella Wells on the phone Mark", Courtney said. "Mikella, I hope you're having a great day", I said. "It is starting off to be a typical Monday morning. What can I do for you Mark", she said. "I need you to fit me into your schedule next week for at least two hours. Let me know when is convenient. We will have a lot to go over", I said. "I will let you know by Wednesday when will be good", she said. "I appreciate your time Mikella", I said.

Sharon from Human Resources called. I let her know the names of some of the people that would come in. I told her I would let her know later on what to pay each of them after she gets her list of who reports. I also asked her to put ads in local newspapers south of the city up to a 100 miles away looking for carpenters, welders and young men and women 18 to 25 years old for security services. I then told Courtney I would be out of the office until about 2 PM.

I left the office and headed for the lab. They were busy building hover carts and ambulance carts. I told them I needed at least 100 generators built about half the size of the cart generators. I told them to make one first and check the electrical strength. I then set them down and told them we would be working on something that is secret. No one is to know what they were working on. It was not to be discussed outside of the lab. If they were not comfortable with it, that they could leave now and I would understand. I filled them in a little about the weapons after I felt they would be with me to the finish. They were excited about having a bunch of drones flying around. I told them we would have a group of drone enthusiasts coming to work with us; that I would like to keep the operation of the anti-gravity units confidential. If they figured it out, so be it. I told them we were building a new lab of fifty thousand square feet used for the drones and later on for another secret project. I called Courtney and told her I could not get back to the office I would be there early in the morning. I left the lab and headed to the Broadside. I needed to speak with Sarah.

I got to the Broadside about 4:30 PM and waited for Sarah to get home. Felicia came running up and gave me a big hug. "How is my new best friend", she said. Two of her brothers came about 15 minutes later. I told them I just needed to speak with their mom for a little bit. Sarah got home about 5 PM. Felicia started dinner and Sarah and I went for a walk. "A couple of things for you Sarah; I have an idea for a coffee shop in the New City. If you would be interested, I could set you up in business. You would hopefully work fewer hours and make more money. I can get you a four bedroom apartment in New City", I said. I told her about the cappuccino and donuts. Most could be sold from the shop and by cart in the Tower. The more I talked the more excited she got. I told her it would take two weeks to get it all setup. That would give you time to give notice to your supervisor. I then told her about Dawn. It really was not my place, but I was thinking about Felicia bumping into her and it might be easier to ease things along. Sarah said she would do whatever she could to be part of her life again. I told her I would see her next week and show her the shop and where she would live. Sarah said that I was not leaving yet, that I had a job to fulfill. She took my hand and guided me into her apartment to the bedroom. After about an hour, I left and headed home.

On the way home, I stopped by Mandy's and told her I would not be seeing her for quite a while. I would work nights and weekends on this new assignment and would not have much time for anything else. I also told her there was a spot for her in medical school if she wanted it. It would be hard going raising 2 children, going to school and working part time, but I knew she could do it. I got home about 8 PM. I was not even hungry. I just locked the door and went to bed.

The next morning driving to the Tower I noticed that about 25% of the dome was already completed and there were already at least a few thousand workers going hard at it. It was looking really nice with that blue plastic mixed in. I only hoped it would work like I had hoped. I did not test the plastic. Everyone seemed to be in a good mood. It was probably all that fresh air they were getting from the opening in the dome. I said hi to everyone and gave Carol and Judy a big hug. I started to give Courtney one, but she sort of backed off. That is okay, I thought. Courtney followed me into the office with her pad ready to write. I gave her a list of things to do. About ten minutes later Sunshine came in with the cappuccino cart and with all smiles. "I thought I would surprise you boss", she said. "You always surprise me Sunshine", I said. She put a cup of cappuccino on my desk and I got up and hugged and thanked her. She said bye and went out and passed out coffee to everyone.

I called Sonia at housing and asked how my new apartment was going. She said I could move in by the end of the week. I had two, two bedroom apartments converted to one. I had the two bathrooms made as one with a large six by four foot shower with two shower heads seven foot high, seats put on each end of shower and a handle to turn to turn of the water jets that would hit from at least a dozen positions at one. The bathtub would be a walk in with jets also. I ordered special furniture from a friend outside. I will have him deliver it Saturday.

Manufacturing is supposed to have me two new security doors delivered today. Security will get me new locks. I want no one coming into my lab I don't know especially when I put the new weapon systems together. It will be hard enough trying to keep it secret from within my group.

I was getting ready to leave and Malcolm from downstairs asked me to drop by his office. He is one of the corporate executives. I had met him and his assistant Mary a few weeks ago in the dining facility. "Mark, I am glad you could stop by", he said. "What can I do for you Malcolm", I reluctantly said. "As you know, I am a corporate executive and my job is to see if everything in the city runs smoothly to corporate standards. You have done some amazing things over the past month and I was wondering if I could get a handle on what you are currently working on", he said. "As you know Malcolm, everything I do is for a reason and generally affects the city or the corporation. I don't feel I have a need to let you or anyone else know what I am working on until I am ready", I said. "Well Mark, you have to tell me. I am your superior and must be updated on all your work. Is that clear?" he said. "Well Malcolm, you are not my superior and I do not have to tell you anything. If you will check I am your superior and I suggest you find yourself something to do before I find you something. Is that very clear?" I said as I got up and walked out. I went back to my office. I called the president's office. His executive assistant said he would be out of the office for a few hours. I told her to leave a message for him if you would. I told her to write, "as, per earlier discussion, I need a check made on Malcolm Guess and his assistant Mary. He is a corporate executive here in the city." That would be all I said. I told Courtney I was going to the lab.

When I got to the lab, everyone was busy as bees. I asked Sunshine to have manufacturing make me a dozen of those coffee carts. I also needed about two dozen square yards of heavy aluminum pans made. I need a dozen of the pans made with heating coils that could warm food, but nothing real hot. Rocky and Sunshine already had some of the new people working on the drones. I figured it a while. As soon as all the parts come in, we will work the long hours. Judy said that it was something she was used to anyway. Rocky complained because it would tie up his weekends, but Sunshine would be here, so it would probably work out. If the rest of the crew coming in would work half as well as these three I thought, I would have the best crew in the country and I could do just about anything.

Over the next week, I had the coffee shop set up for Sarah and her family. She would have her kids working in the shop part-time. The day they opened for business and served the first pot of cappuccino, the word got around quickly. Sarah was brewing cappuccino as fast as she could and was selling donuts out every day before lunch. She went to work at 4 AM, opened at 6 AM, closed at noon and went home at 1PM. She was now working fewer hours, had more time with her family and everyone seemed to be a lot happier. I even hear that Dawn and Felicia were talking. I was hoping they would get together.

CHAPTER 15   A Month Of Celebration

A few weeks had passed and the dome over the city was half finished. It was looking good. Things slowed on the dome because of the hurricane that came in on Boone City. Most of the materials for the dome were sent down to Boone. Nearly a thousand people lost their lives when part of the dome collapsed. That is a big city of nearly three million people. A good part of Houston moved there when the new dome was first built. It was supposed to be safer. Antonio manufacturing has nearly tripled their facility in the last month or so. We had products coming to us faster now. I was thinking how great these people worked compared to the people in 2017 in my other conscious. People were not lazy and expected something for doing nothing.

I have nearly twenty people now working on drones. We have already trained the young security cadets to fly the drones. They are taking to it like video games. Once they become efficient, we will train with weapons. That scares me. I am hoping they don't wipe each other out. I have secured a place in west Texans to use as a firing range. Antonio City built a complex out there so the cadets will have a place to train, sleep and eat. I will train 75 cadets to use the smaller drones and 15 of the best to fly the larger drones. I flew one drone out over the Gulf Sea at 35,000 feet and fired a blaster for about three minutes. It nearly shut down. It took too much power from the anti-gravity disk. I brought it back and increased the size of the generator by fifty percent and sent it out again. I could fire the blaster up to fifteen minutes without it losing power. I had a winner, I thought.

I had promised many people a celebration when the dome was finished. The dome would not be completed because of Boone City. I need to have the celebration before the weather change. The celebration would be partially inside and out. I just want to make sure we don't go into a rainy season and rain the celebration out. I contacted bands to come in a play for a day. The corporation put up money to buy all the food we needed for barbecue, and other food and beverages needed to make it a hit. What scared me was how many people would attend. We have two million people in the city. We should serve food and whatever until it runs out and dance the night away, I thought. Big Mike and a group of cooks volunteered to help out. I had over 550 barbecue pits made. I was thinking this would be the biggest party in the history of this world and mine. I asked the contractors to build ten stages. They had it done in a day. I ordered speaker systems. It was hard to find some decent speakers. It seemed like everyone volunteered to help out. The service people got out and cleared acres of land to make it comfortable.

I thought about how the kids were going to really love this outing. Then an idea popped into my head. I could get all the students to sing a song or songs during the celebration. I contacted Betty Morgan, Director of Education. She thought it would be a great idea if someone could get all those children together to sing a song. I told her I would take care of it. Just let the schools know that I will be in contact with them. We had a lot of schools and a lot of kids. I called the schools and talked to the principles. I ask them to get at least five hundred volunteers to sing at the celebration. I told them I would get copies of a song and send it over so the kids could start learning it. I called Courtney and asked her to call a printer and have enough copies made for all the schools. I called the conductor of the orchestra and ask if they would play songs for the celebration including the one for the children. I also needed some of their orchestra's to practice with the children before.

It is a pretty day outside the dome. The children had already started to show up. I don't know if anyone can imagine it. There were approximately 25,000 kids that showed up to sing. I guess when I said 500 from each school; I did not figure it in for 50 schools. I did the best I could to split them up so I could have different groups singing different parts of the song. People from the orchestra set up in the middle of everyone. There were about 100,000 people including the children all around now. I had already written the music for the orchestra and they had practiced the song before coming. I gave each of the groups of children numbers, so when I flagged a number, they would sing their part. I was getting so excited to hear what the outcome of what was about to happen. I flipped on the speakers and the orchestra played. I then started the children singing. I sang a few lines solo with some children backup. I could hear some stumbling at first, but the children did well for a first time. We practiced the song five more times. The families around were applauding. You could hear some pointing out their children. It was amazing.

When the day came of the celebration, the beer trucks rolled in about 4 AM followed by food trucks. We had huge coolers set up to put the food in. I found out from the Pub how they made their refrigeration for the beers. It worked well in large areas. We could cool a lot of beverages. People showed up out of the woodwork. It looked like we would have everyone volunteering. My worries about a failure faded. Everyone was chipping in. There were about a thousand portable restrooms set up around the area.

Randy Morgan and his band came in about 9 AM. I got with him and went over about sixty songs as quickly as I could. I had written out sheet music on about half of them. I told Randy I would sing with them and that we had to move to ten different stages during the day. He did not have a problem with it. We practiced the different songs. Randy told me if I were to join the band we could make millions selling records all over the world. I did not say no, I just told him I had things to do for the corporation first. Most of the songs styles were a lot different from this world. I had a few problems with some of the songs because the wording. Some of the places in this world exists but under different names. I just changed the names.

People came in by the thousands. They were bringing blankets to spread on the ground, picnic baskets and ice chests. The Governor and his group came in and situated him close to the main stage. Have you ever stepped on an ant bed? It looked that like here. It looked like you could not get another person in here, yet they kept coming. It was 11 AM and the Governor got up on the main stage with the LT Governor. He made a short speech welcoming everyone to the celebration and to enjoy. A few minutes later, you could hear the bands on the other stages play. I got up on stage with Randy and we played. The whole area was popping with people dancing, yelling, talking loud and just plain enjoying themselves. At noon time, I announced there were free beer and other beverages until they were gone. It was then a race to the coolers. It was just about 1PM and I announced that we had a special presentation for everyone to enjoy. All the speakers from the different stages went live on one setting. The children got up on the stages and all around the stages. Some people started applauding. The orchestra set up nearly square in the middle of the crowd. The orchestra played and I sang "We Are The World." When the children started singing, the whole crowd stopped to listen. The children really sounded wonderful. The speakers were set up where you could hear all of them at once but also some of the speakers were local. It made it sound like surround sound and a little echo all at once. The song lasted for about five minutes. That is longer than any song in this world. When the children finished, the crowd roared. They were such a great hit. I could not have asked for anything better for this crowd. I went on singing off and on through the day and into the night. People from the outside were still coming in through the day. It seemed like you could see people for miles. We ran out of beer about 6 PM. You could hear complaints from the crowd, but that stopped when I announced the barbecue was ready and the food was free while it lasted. Everyone started clamoring to the pits. The bands played until 7 PM and took an hour break. The cooks saved the band members something to eat. I had brought a cooler for the band members with all the beer and beverages they could drink. About 7:30 PM another beer truck pulled in. People drank the beer before it even went in the coolers. At 8 PM, the children got up and sang "We Are The World" again. At 9 PM, I announced the end of the celebration and that I hoped everyone had a good time and thank them for coming.

A couple of weeks after the celebration, Sonia Weis, Director of Housing announced at a meeting there were about 15,000 new applications for housing in the city. All the apartments were already filled. John Ryan said that he had already cleared the area for building another portion of the city, but it would take about four months to get all the cubicles in and stacked because of what happened in Boone City. They were still replacing cubicles. Antonio City was also building a new portion of their city. The Governor announced that since the new buses have been running and he guessed because of the celebration that business has gone up ten folds in the city. Profits were soaring and the board of directors were thrilled with what we had done here. I was also supposed to commend Mark for his fine work here in the city since he came to us. Everyone applauded me. I thanked them for all their support or none of it would have happened.

Another couple of months had passed and Boone city finally had their dome repaired with the new framing from the alloy and the plastic. At least a tenth of their city was somewhat safe now. The board of directors said that they would get a new dome on the rest of the city after Capital City and Antonio City was completed. I just hoped they would not have another storm until then. Profits were up for the corporation, but the board of directors were looking for new revenues. Texans had already taken in the territories of Colorado, Kansas, Nebraska and Southern Dakota. I told the board where to find gold quantities in the Round Rock, western Texans, old New Mexico area, Colorado and Southern Dakota. Texans was selling out more resources to other countries it was purchasing. With some countries, it was a matter of barter rather than to trade for gold or other precious metals. I had also suggested that we build a pipeline using the plastic to make the pipeline. The pipeline would extend from the Orleans River to the desert of West Texas. Orleans River in this world is the Mississippi. North of the Tennessee Territories, it is called the Great Chicago River. Making a lake in the desert would allow that whole area to be built up for future population and if needed, water reserve for Antonio City. The board of directors agreed to start building the pipeline this next spring. The water siphoned from the river would be only in the spring time or when flood water was coming from the north. That way, it would not upset the French who use that waterway for shipping out of New Orleans. I also suggested building more dams along the Nevada River.

December had come around and everyone was getting excited about the New Years. In Texans, New Years is a big celebration. They exchange gifts and party. Much like what we did for Christmas in one of my lives. Close to the end of December decorations went up around the city and the whole country. The stores were full of merchandise waiting for the big rush. We had all the drones ready and all the cadets were trained to fly them, so I gave everybody off a week to enjoy the coming New Years.

I still had six light cannons to build and thought this would be a good time to work on them with no one around. Judy stuck by me helping me wire the cannons. I knew something was coming and I needed to be ready for it.

CHAPTER 16 War

January came and went without incident. It was the morning of February 6^{th,} 1990. It is Thursday morning. "The President is on the line Mark", Courtney said with a smile. She has been getting nice lately. She even hugs me now when I come in. She is really a beautiful lady. If only she did not work with me, I think sometimes. "What can I do for you Mr. President?" I asked. "Besides commending you again on all that you do Mark, I need to make you aware of some circumstances that are currently happening. We arrested and executed more than a dozen spies over the last few months. I just talked with the President of the United States again. They know we are trying to take up the last remaining part of the Dakotas and that it would split this continent mostly in our favor. Some of the US settlements were in the areas we brought into Texans. Their president says that their generals are getting real nervous and want to do something about it. We have never worried much about our security because of our alliance with France, China and Japan. My concern is that if the US ever wanted to do something, it would take a while before our allies could get any help here to protect us. France only has about 25,000 troops in Orleans. I just want you to be aware and possibly hire more security and training them with firearms. I will try to triple the guard we have", he said. "Mr. President, I have been working on a way to secure our country. As I have already told you, I will not discuss it with anyone. You will just have to trust me. You know everything that I have done for this country; I have done for a reason to benefit it. Just try to give me a heads up if anything were to happen," I said. "Are you aware Mark that the

US has a pretty good size army and they have a navy with an aircraft carrier", he said. "I did not know about the fleet, but I suspected it Mr. President", I said. "I spoke with the commanding representative from Orleans and he told me that they could commit up to 25,000 troops, but it would take at least a day or more to get them in any position to help. We have no air force. We have never needed it. The US has jets and bombers", he said. "I am preparing for any type of invasion", I said. "That does not help assure me. That is a lot to take in when you cannot see what you are talking about", he said. He hung up and I went back to doing paper work I was getting behind on.

I got on the phone and ordered six large trucks. I had already worked on setting up more transmitters with greater range to fly my drones. I needed to be sure that my cadets could do what they were trained to do. I already had six guys I trusted to fire the cannons and six others as drivers. Only the people that fired the cannons knew what they were for though. Everything else has been kept secret or at least I believe a secret. I should have the cannons completely finished by the end of the month. I just had to believe that nothing would happen until then. I am just hoping that everything will work like I wanted it to. After the Thursday staff meeting, I went back to the lab. Judy was working on the light cannons. I went straight to the drafting room. About 6 PM, I heard banging at the door. I ask who was at the door through the intercom. It was a lady from security. I opened the door and stepped out. "I was told that there were going to be possible problems in the city. Security will need access to your buildings, so we can monitor happenings going on", she said. "Who gave you that order?" I asked. "Gene the new supervisor did", she said. I ask for his number and called him. I told him that if he sent anyone else down to my buildings checking on anything that I did, he would be arrested for treason. I did not hear any more of him.

It was the sixteenth of March. It was actually a pleasant day outside after the cold winter we had gone through. It was sure nice to have those generators in place or this and probably the other cities would be without power for days at a time. I entered my office about 7 AM. Sarah had already been in the office with her coffee and donuts. I had arranged to have coffee and donuts on my desk every morning. I paid her for a full year, not to forget me. Courtney came in and gave me a big hug. This hug was one of those loving hugs. "What's up?" I said. "Nothing, I just need someone to hug me", she said and sat down with a pad in hand ready to write. She had been getting awfully friendly lately, I thought. I started to give her a list of things to do when the phone rang. It is the President", Courtney said. "Mark, I just got a call from the new President of the United States. He was one of their big generals before he got elected." He was stuttering and I could hear the fear in his voice. "He has given us six hours to surrender our country or they will take it from us no matter what the cost of lives. He said they were not happy with us splitting this continent in half and it was causing security problems. In six hours, he will send a jet to each of our cities and fire rockets. He said maybe with the damage; and a large number of the people dead, any thoughts of holding out would be delusional. Our allies could not back us up for days except for Orleans, but they only have about 25,000 troops. We do not have any force that could even sway them", he said. "Mr. President, if their president or general calls again, please let me handle them. Have all calls directed to me", I said. "I trust you Mark", he said and hung up.

All my cadets had nothing to do but practice flying the drones. My transmitters were all online. I called my six guys to meet me in my main lab that could fire the cannon. My trucks were already parked out in front and fueled up. I told my six guys, Judy, Sunshine and Rocky about the upcoming possibility of war. Rocky asked if he could take the cannon to Boone City. His parents lived in old Houston. I had complete confidence in Rocky. My drivers soon came in and I had help from the guys from the drone lab help in loading and setting the cannons. I sent two cannons to Dal City, two to Boone City, and one to Antonio City. They were to position themselves about five miles out. I had the cadets that were going to help me with the large drones report to the transmitter room close to security headquarters. Judy and Sunshine would supervise the other cadets on attacking with the smaller drones. My drones took off to the Gulf Sea. The other drones took off to the Texans northeast border.

About three hours had passed. I was getting nervous. I guess you could say scared. I have never been even in a fight in my life, I thought. I could see the carrier fleet on screen now. I flew my done to 35,000 feet directly above the fleet. The other drones hovered about two thousand feet over the sea about five miles away. Judy called and told me that the monitors show a lot of tanks, cannons and soldiers on the border. There were a lot of trucks coming in, some with troops. One blast from one of the small drones could put a hole about the size of a baseball through their hulls. The larger drones I commanded could put a hole about the size of a large medicine ball in the ships we were about to attack. A call came into the transmitter room transferred from the Tower. It was General Reinhart, commander of the US military. "I was told that you were the Texans' commander. You have about three hours to consider Mr. Anglin before I commit my troops. I would rather there not cause damage to property and loss of life if at all possible", he said. I could see on the monitor that a jet took off the deck of the carrier and others were getting ready to take off. "General, if one more jet takes off from your carrier, I will have your fleet destroyed. Look to the sea", I said. I was hoping he thought we had a submarine or something in the water and not look up and out. "How could you know we had launched a jet? You do not have a navy or air force. It must be those damned French", he said. Another jet took off the carrier. I was handling the controls of the drone at 35,000 thousand feet. At this height, it would take in about a mile in circumference. The beam would not immediately pierce the decks of the ships, but it would melt any rubber, light metal, glass or plastic. Any paper would ignite and anyone caught in the beam would be dead in about a minute from their blood boiling and burning of the skin. I had about fifteen minutes on the gun. I opened it up full and fired directly above the carrier. The jet taking off crashed into the water about five miles away. I told the cadets to fire on the supporting ships at the water level if possible and sink all the ships then fire on the carrier. The general on the line said, "what the hell" and the line went dead. We sank all the ships in about fifteen minutes. The carrier took about an hour to finally disappear beneath the waves. I told my cadets handling the large drones to head due east to the Atlantic. One of the destroyers got off a few missiles and took out three of my drones. So we headed to the Atlantic with twelve drones. Judy had given the order to fire on the troops at the border when they started to cross. The drones were firing from one and two miles out and were not touched by any fire from the US. Sunshine commanded another fifteen cadets with more drones heading due northeast. If there were any reinforcements, she would contain them. When my drones got to the Atlantic, they flew directly north at about fifty feet above the water. I was not sure if they had radar and was not going to take any chances.

Judy's drones took out all their heavy stuff. Most of the troops were retreating. Sunshine called and said that she could see about 35 or 40 aircraft flying toward Texans about 500 miles out. They were being accompanied by six jet aircraft. I told her to take out the six jets first and then work on the bombers or support aircraft, whatever they were. The US did not know what hit them. They have seen nothing like our weapons. All they saw was light and bang, they were dead. The phone rang and it was General Reinhart again. "I don't know what you have Mr. Anglin, but this has got to stop. I have given orders to pull back my troops", he said. I just let him talk for a while. Sunshine said the aircraft were still coming south. "General, I told you not to let anymore jets take off. General, if you were serious about your troops pulling back, why is there a squadron of aircraft with jet escort flying toward Texans?" I asked. "There must be a mistake on your part Mr. Anglin, I have recalled all troops since you took out the fleet", he said. "Your troops crossed the Texans border after the fleet sank General", I said. I let the planes fly about another twenty miles west. "Well, they are still coming General and now they are gone", I said. "Wait, he said. I hung up the phone. Sunshine's group attacked the jets. She lost eight drones but was able to destroy the squadron. "Boss, you would not believe what I am looking at. There are thousands of parachutes of all colors filling the sky. Some are on fire. It looks pretty", she said. She sounded like she was having the time of her life. "Do you want me to fire on the soldiers", she asked. "No Sunshine let them go. I would bet as they hit the ground, they are running back home. Judy reported that large groups of troops were waving white flags. She started laughing. "We do not even have anyone to take them prisoner."

These large drones fly at over a thousand miles an hour. We were getting close to the northeast portion of the US. General Reinhardt came on the phone again. "I told you that all troops have been told to return. Let's get this little skirmish resolved", he said. "You call it a little skirmish when you lost an entire fleet and most of your troops and armament. If you would have attacked us, we would have lost possibly millions because our cities are so compacted. You want us to quit because you can't play ball anymore. You got an injury, so it is over. Well General, I need assurances that you will not try anything like this again and I want the other nations to know if they tried anything like this, they would be destroyed. I have to set an example to make sure it does not happen again", I said. He hung up. About fifteen minutes later the President called. Mark, the United States said they would stop the war if we did. They would make whatever concessions we wanted. You have them scared to death", he said. "Mr. President, we cannot let them get away with this. If we set no example, they or someone else will try it thinking we are weak. I will finish this. When I get through, you can ask for any concessions you want. I need to get back to things sir. I will speak with you in a little while", I said. I had forgotten about the cannons I sent out to the different cities. We did not have communications with the trucks, so I will just have to wait for them to report. Sunshine's was still heading northeast, but nothing to report.

My group headed in toward land. I could see a naval base on the monitor. I wonder if that was the naval base in Virginia. There were about 25 ships. We fired on the ships. Most were not even manned. We sunk every one without any losses. We headed north to Washington, D.C. It looked like a city of about two million people. It was nothing like our cities. It was so spread out like our old cities. I took my drone up to about 35,000 thousand feet directly above the capital. I guess they had radar. Jets came out of nowhere coming straight for my drone. There were about thirty jets in the air. The drones attacked the jets heading up toward my drone and taking them out with one blast one by one. When it was over, I had five drones left counting mine. I opened my beam on the capital. You could see the smoke, then the fire erupt from the capital building. All the buildings around it burned. The other four drones were taking out targets of opportunity. It was sad there was such a loss of life, but I had to make sure they did not come back again. I called the President and let him know that now he could talk concessions if he wanted to. I called back all our drones. The people in the country did not even know what had happened. It never made it to their backyards.

It was about an hour later when the President called. "Did you hear about Boone City Mark? Apparently they got attacked by one jet. I don't know what you did Mark or how you did it but, you killed their president and his whole cabinet. I was also told that they thought that there was a loss of over a million people in your attacks. Please remind me not to ever get you mad", he said. "I told you Mr. President that I was working on something secret", I said. "They want to send a delegation to Antonio City to talk concessions. I told them we would not attack anymore if the meeting was successful", he said. "Good answer. Keep them on the defensive", I said. "I want to make sure you will be available for the meeting", he said. "I will meet with their delegation, but it had better be a delegation that can make a decision on the spot and not one where they will have to go home and think it over", I said. "I will let them know Mark. I want to see you as soon as possible when you get done", he said. "Okay, maybe tomorrow", I said. Our guys that manned the cannons called in. I told them all to come home. Rocky finally called in a said he shot down a jet, but it still crashed into Boone City. It must have been that first jet that took off that we missed, I thought. "Just get yourself home Rocky, someone here is really nervous to see you", I said. "Okay boss", he said. Sunshine calling me boss caught on to a lot of the people working with me.

The Governor called me to his office. He did not understand what was happening. He did not understand what we had done. The President had filled him in on what he knew. "Why didn't you fill me in on what was really happening out there? We could have had loss of lives and damage here in the city", he said. "If I would have told you Governor, what could you have done, other than maybe slowed me down so I could not do what I needed to do right away", I said. I could have evacuated the city," he said. "If you would have attempted to evacuate two million people in less than six hours, it would have been a miracle. And besides, how many people would have died tromping on each other trying to get out the door?" I asked. "Maybe you're right Mark, but I still think I should have known. Hell people in security knew more than I did", he said. "I am going to Antonio City in the morning and will be back late in the afternoon. We should have a meeting of the directors", I said. "I will make it happen", he said grunting.

"I heated up your cappuccino for you", Courtney said as I entered the office. "Thank you Courtney", I said as I sat down totally exhausted. Courtney sat down on the couch next to me. "I did not say anything to anyone. I knew you wanted to keep it all secret", she said. She leaned forward and wrapped her arms around my neck. She gave me a light kiss on the neck and then hugged me. "I will take care of you", she said. I don't know if I am reading anything into what just happen, but I had better watch my step, I thought. I thanked her again and told her I had to go back to the lab.

Judy had called everyone to the drone lab working with us except the few that were out of town. Sunshine had called the pub and they brought over all the beer they had in their cooler. "I know you don't approve of drinking on the job Mark, but we are here to congratulate you on what just happened. Besides you can blame the beer on Sunshine. She bought all that club had", Judy said. We partied into the evening. "If anyone is early for work tomorrow, they are fired", I said jokingly.

CHAPTER 17   Concessions

The next morning I got in my truck and drove to Antonio City. What a beautiful day for a ride, I thought. I got into the city about 9 AM. They had a cart waiting for me. When I got to the tower, there were people standing all around. Some that knew who I was clapped and patting me on the back saying hello. I went up to the executive suites. It looked like everyone was waiting for me here also. The whole office rose and was applauding me. The President came out and shook my hand and put his arm on my shoulder and guided me into his office. He took me over to the lounge area. "How would you like an office here?" he asked. "I appreciate the thought sir, but I am happy where I am for now. Your security director called up here and told her boss what basically happened, Mark. That is how everyone knew before you got here", he said. "What I did and what she knew was supposed to be secret. When I get back to Capital City, Mikella will be looking for a new position", I said. "Oh, come on Mark, mellow out", he said. "Mr. President, secrets are supposed to be just that. If we tell everyone what we are doing before they need to know, we could be open to most anything and security for one will mean absolutely nothing", I said. "You are right of course Mark. Let's get down to business", he said. The Washington delegation will be here on Sunday evening. I figured to have the meetings starting Monday morning if that is all right with you", he said. "Monday will be fine Mr. President. Have you and the board thought about what you would ask in the peace treaty?" I asked. "Not really, I was waiting to speak with you first", he said. "Is what I say that important?" I asked. The board leans heavily on what you say.

They know what you have in your head. I don't think even want to buck you in any way. They even have thoughts of making you the CEO of the board", he said. "I can tell you, I do not want that job", I said. "You pretty much already run the country", he said. "I wouldn't go that far, I said.

"Tell the US that we want Missouri, Iowa, and Minnesota territories without any squabbling. Missouri has large deposits of iron, copper, gold and silver. Iowa has great farming and Missouri has large amounts or iron plus other resources. These are all US Territories they have not brought into their union. The territories must also agree to come into Texans to make this possible. We need no uprising on our hands. This will give Texans a lot of resources to keep us in high profits for years to come, plus the taxes from individuals and businesses. I really don't mean to sound ruthless, but the US brought this upon themselves. If they do not concede, we have the ability to destroy the entire United States. They still do not know what kind of a weapon we have and I will not tell anyone, not even you sir", I said. "I understand Mark", he said. "Another thing they had better understand. "If we find even one of their spies here in Texans, we will execute them and it would be a declaration of war", I said. "Would you like to talk to the board?" he said. They will all be here by tomorrow", he said. "No, I will see them all next Monday, I am sure. "It is sure to be an exciting meeting", he said. I will be here on Sunday if you need to go over anything with me before your meeting, let me know", I said.

I returned to Capital City and informed the Governor and directors what happened and what would happen. I also fired the security director. I think everyone left the meeting scared but relieved.

Sunday came fairly quickly. I entered Antonio City about 2 PM. The guest house they gave me was meant for a king. It was the most gorgeous room I have ever seen. It was way out of my league, I thought. An office boy showed up with a note to meet the President at 4 PM. I entered the office a little early. It looked like a normal day of work with all office staff and executives on hand. Everyone seemed glad to see me. They told me to go right into the President's office. There were about twenty people in the office. The President introduced me to the board of directors. There were board members representing a lot of countries. I did not realize how many countries owned Texans. It is a wonder anyone would have attacked Texans. The US probably was not aware of the board, I thought. After about an hour with the board, it came to me that these people were probably the top richest people in the world. We went over a good bit of what we would talk about tomorrow and then went to dinner. The dining facility had a large spread waiting for us when we entered. After dinner about half of us went up to the club for some drinks. There were twelve men and women from the US delegation sitting at a table across the floor. I stood up and went over to the table. I introduced myself and told them I would see them in the morning. After about an hour, the President talked me into singing a few songs. That is one thing I love more than anything. I think I was born on the stage sometimes. Laughing to myself, I was thinking with one of my other personalities I never had time for anything like this. About 10PM I said my goodnights and went back to my room at the guest house.

6 AM came early it seemed. I got dressed and went to breakfast. I think everyone was here. I was invited to sit with the President, his wife and Sandra. Sandra seemed excited to see me. After breakfast the President and I headed down to his office. We discussed more about the meeting. It finally came to

me that the President did not really run this country. He was given orders and he followed them to the letter. He is like what we used to say about the presidents from my other world. That the presidents are all pawns just following orders. We headed down to the conference room. This conference room took up nearly the entire floor. The table could sit seventy or eighty people easily. Each chair had a glass, picture of water and note pad on the table. I sat down at the head of the table and the President sat at the other head. Board members filled one side of the table and the delegation at on the other. The board wanted me to run the meeting.

The President stood up and said, "let's bring this meeting to order. We are probably going to be here awhile. Will the US delegation introduce themselves and let us know your capacity", he said. They made their introductions and the board made theirs. One of the delegate members stood and said, "we would like to first speak about what we need to negotiate." I stood up and said, "I did not introduce myself, I am Mark Anglin. There will be no negotiations at this meeting. You are here to accept concessions." One of the members said that I was just a boy. "This boy is the one that defeated your navy and army Miss", I said. There were no other objections. I told the delegation what we wanted to make a peace treaty. They mumbled to each other. "It is plain and simple ladies and gentlemen. You started a war and lost. Now you will either concede to our conditions or your country will be destroyed. It will not be destroyed by any of our allies; it will be destroyed by our resources. Do you want to take that chance?" I said. "No", the lady that seemed to be a leader said. "We will listen to what you have to say Mr. Anglin", she said. "This is going to be cut and dried. We are asking you to give us the US Territories Missouri, Iowa and Minnesota. Also, the leaders and citizens of those territories will need to tell us that they agree to be part of Texans. If anyone of them says no, there will be no peace. I want you to understand something else. You know we have uncovered many of your spies in our cities. If you have any spies left here, you had better tell them to leave immediately. If we find any US spies, we will execute them and the peace treaty will be null and void and I promise we will attack you and we will be merciless. In our country, we have little crime and disturbances, so our security force and army is small. That is why a lot of countries think we are weak. You have found out the hard way we are not weak. To let you know and I am sure you already understand that if we asked, we could get what military we need from our allies to destroy you if we failed. Now back to the question at hand. Do you agree to the terms which I have given you? Also, you have ninety days to complete this arrangement, so I would suggest no dolling around", I said. They mumbled between themselves again. The head lady said that "I guess we have to agree to your terms Mr. Anglin. Draw up whatever paperwork you need and we will all sign it." We have already drawn up the agreement with your names on the agreement. You have only to sign it. The President and I will be the only ones signing for the Corporation", I said. One of the executive assistants brought over the agreement and put it in front of the delegates. They went over the agreement for about a half hour then signed it. "I actually thought you were going to balk or make excuses. I am glad we did not have to go through that. You would have been very unhappy with your trip here. This has been one of the shortest meetings and one of the most important that I have been to since I have been with the Corporation. When it is time for lunch, we can all set at one community table or you can sit alone; your option. We can sit here now and discuss whatever you would like", I said. We talked for about two hours on what ifs and went to lunch. We had a nice luncheon. The delegates left about 1:30 PM to the airport. We had another meeting after lunch. The board asked me questions about my weapon and possibly what would be the next surprise. I told them the weapon was secret from everyone. I told my people that if they mentioned it to anyone, they could be executed for treason. Once you let out a secret, it seems everyone soon finds out about it and usually the wrong people", I said. As for new projects, I am sure I will come up with something as soon as I feel the cities or the Corporation are in need of it. We must work the resources in those new territories as soon as possible. There is a lot of wealth out there. Also, I believe we need to break down our country into states like the US and Mexico. People will fight for a country. People will fight even harder for a state they live in because it is home. Those citizens also must understand that they are not part of the US, that they live in a corporate country and have to follow different rules. They could either follow our rules or leave the country", I said. "We will discuss everything you said Mark and will come to a conclusion by the end of this week", one of the directors said. One of the directors said, "since you will not accept CEO, how would you feel about building your own city. You can name it Anglin City if you like Mark", she said. "I will keep that in mind. I just need to make sure I finish up whatever it is I need to do before I take on something else, thank you", I said. I left the tower and headed home.

CHAPTER 18   The New Texans

The US waited the whole ninety days to turn over the three territories to us. They were very polite about it I heard. It would be interesting on how their citizens would take being in the Corporation. I am not sure if the people expect to have the Corporation take care like the US did. We have no welfare here. If you do not work, you do not eat. People unable to take care of themselves would be taken care off and old people will always have the best of whatever is available. If they like socialism, they need to move out of the country.

The Corporation assembled a group of people to work on making states break down Texans. They came up with twelve states; Texas, New Mexico, Oklahoma, Arkansas, Missouri, Colorado, Iowa, Kansas, Nebraska, South Dakota, Minnesota and North Dakota. The United States of Texans has a good ring.

It was not long and we had governments from all over the world wanting to buy whatever weapon we had that defeated the United States military. We just told them, it was not for sale. We also told them that if they sent any spies to find out about the weapon, it would be a declaration of war and they would not want to consider that at all. That seemed to cool every ones heals.

With all that was going on, I could not enjoy my new apartment. When I went home, it was to sleep or I stayed at Judy's. I went home and took a look at how it looked. The furniture was the fanciest I could find. Any lady would die for my bathroom, I thought. I had a walk in closet the size of a bedroom. My bedroom was about twice the size of any other bedroom in the city. I had one extra bedroom in case I had a guest. I laid down for a light rest and fell asleep. Knocking on door woke me up. "Can we talk Mark", Dawn said. "What do you need Dawn?" I asked. When she walked in and saw my apartment, she made comments on how pretty everything was and was looking at everything. She sat down on the couch and started talking. "I need to know why you are mad at me", she said. "I am not mad of you Dawn", I said. "Why did you treat me like a one night stand and never contact me", she said. "Dawn, you never stopped to consider what was going on in my life. You sort of forced yourself on me for one. I already had two ladies that I was seeing and you probably haven't heard yet, but I was preparing for an attack by the United States. We stopped their attack and have since made peace. It was probably the shortest war in history", I said. "I did not know, I just thought you really liked me and as hard as I tried not to, I fell in love with you. I am really sorry", she said as she got up and headed to the door. "Dawn, wait. I really do like you and you are probably one of the most beautiful ladies in this whole city. Please stay and we can talk", I said. I was wondering if I was making another mistake. I was still seeing Judy off and on. "Where are you working now Dawn?" I asked. "I am an executive assistant on the 38th floor. It is not as exciting as working for you, but it is alright, she said. "I am glad you are working", I said. "I saw that new assistant of yours. I hate her; she is so beautiful. I bet you have a hard time keeping focused", she said. "Like you were dawn; I think about the beauty, but also she is my assistant. I cannot mess with my assistants. It is hard enough working with Judy. To let you know also Dawn, I will leave in probably a few weeks and heading to the territories up north. With the peace treaties, we took in new territories from the United States", I said. "How long will you be gone", she said. "It is hard to tell. It could be a long time", I said. Dawn put her arms around me and gave me a hug then kissed me on the side of the face working to my lips. She took my hand and pulled me toward the bedroom. She had a black jumpsuit on with a zipper down the front. When she unzipped the suit, she had to squeeze out of it because it was so tight. She had no underwear on and her 38 breasts just popped out. Her perfect body was so hard to resist. We made love for about an hour and then took a shower. She must have raved for thirty minutes about the bathroom. "Can we go dancing", she said. "I guess so Dawn", I said. She went to her apartment to change and came right back over in a beautiful evening dress. She was really a knockout, I thought. I put on a coat and tie and we flew to the Tower in my Hover Car. Dawn had not flown in one and was nervous. The club had many people for a weeknight. We ordered a couple beers. They have the new refrigeration unit now and the beers are ice cold. Dawn was an excellent dancer and we tore up the floor. Cody with the band waved at me to come over. Dawn and I walked across the floor. "Let me ask you something Cody", I was wondering if you would like me to write you some songs. I can write the music for guitar and piano. The cello and drums would have to key in", I said. "That would great", Cody said. "Let's get together tomorrow and we can go over some music", I said. I sang a few songs and Dawn and I went back out on the dance floor. I ordered finger foods when we got back to the table since I had not eaten yet. We left about 11 PM and went to my place.

I woke up at 6 AM. My mind clicked again as I sat on the couch. I was thinking about immigration from the United States. There middle and upper class was supporting half the population of people who did not want to work. If I was in their place and saw where I could benefit by moving to Texans, I think I would pack up my family and move. Why would they want to keep supporting half the nation? I just knew it would happen. My feelings have not been wrong, I thought to myself. We need to get something setup now to accept these people and be able to screen them so we don't get possible trouble makers. I guess that is going to be my next goal. I need to talk to my guys and gals and see who wants to go to the new territories. I will offer double wages to all that go. I will talk with Human Resources about getting them all bonuses like I promised.

The next morning I went to the lab first. I told Sunshine, Judy and Rocky I needed them to help me dismantle the weapons. We would also give the small drones without weapons to security. They could use them to monitor the city. I told Sunshine and Rocky I would like them to go with me to the territories. I told them I would pay them 140,000 credits each. Judy I was thinking could work with me in just about anything I do. She was smart enough to stand in for me if I needed her. I ask Judy if she would like to go to the club with me. I told her about helping the band with some new songs and it could give us a little time to talk. We have not really had much time together for a while. I left the lab and went to the Tower.

When I got to the Tower, I saw the Presidents entourage. I knew he had to be around somewhere. I went by Judy and Carol's desk to say good morning and give them a hug. Carol handed me my pay stub and told me that the President was waiting in my office. I went to my office. I entered the office and the President and one of the board members were sitting in my lounge area drinking cappuccino. "We love this new coffee you came up with Mark. How come we did not get it in Antonio City?" he asked. "I had just finished creating the process when the war started. I just did not really have time to do anything about it", I said. "Well, we want it in Antonio City", he said. I will get someone to get you a cappuccino machine and have them show someone in your city how to make and supply it to the public like we do. We have one lady that has a shop that sells and delivers the coffee and donuts every morning", I said. "We need to talk some business", the President said. "What's up Mr. President?" I said. "With the new territories and all of those new people, we need to come up with something to educate them about the corporate ways. We need to set up manufacturing and mining of the natural resources you vaguely discussed", he said. "I sense another problem also Mr. President. The middle and upper class in the United States are probably now looking at us since the war. It is hard to cover up the loss of over a million citizens. I believe that they will find out that we could offer them a much better life than what they have in their country; especially since they support about half the people in that country who don't want to work. Question will arise on an immigration policy where we need to educate these people of our laws and weeding through any possibilities of trouble makers. I do not know how many people we have that can read minds. Those people would be perfect to interview any people immigrating", I said. "It seems we are going to have a lot of work to do Mark. I hope you will stick with us through this ordeal. This could take a long time to accomplish", he said. "I will start working on organizing teams that might want to volunteer to go to those new territories. As soon as a team gets into the territory, they will need to hire and build cities and an infrastructure. We need at the same time to mine those resources for capital", I said. "That is why you should be the CEO", the director said. "Give me a few weeks gentlemen to put a plan together and I will get right back to you", I said. They said they would speak with the Governor and LT Governor and head back to Antonio City.

I went to my desk and wrote things I needed to remember. I saw that envelope of my pay stub and curiosity got the best of me. When I open it my jaw dropped to the desk. I had over fifty million credits. Dang the corporation must think I am some superman, I thought. I called Courtney on the intercom to tell Carol we need to set a meeting for tomorrow rather than Thursday for the directors. It was very important that everyone attend. I told her I had to go to the lab and left the office. I told Judy I needed to see her in the draft room. When she came in I started letting her in on things that were needed to do and wanted to know if she would stick with me through all this work. I asked her how much money she would like to make over the next year. She kiddingly said at least a million. I told her seriously that it would be no problem. She just looked at me for a while trying to figure out if I was serious or not, then gave me a big hug. She said she would do anything I ask and would travel wherever I wanted her to. I told her I needed her to come to the corporate meeting tomorrow.

I left and went over to the other lab. A lot of the guys were just sitting around doing nothing much. I ask if anyone wanted to volunteer to go to another territory and work. I would find them jobs that matched their expertise. Six of them said they would go. I told them that Sunshine and Rocky would be their supervisors and that I would be getting back to them before the end of the week.

I headed back over to the Tower. Carol asked me to go in the Governor's office. Jerry was sitting in front of the Governor's desk. "Mark, have a seat", he said. "Hi Jerry", I said. "Hey Mark", he said. "The President is telling me that you will be helping with setting up the new territories. I would guess that means taking some of our citizens to help you", he said. "I will not be taking that many, Governor. I will probably take about fifty volunteers from some divisions and a few out of the minor divisions. We will go into one territory at a time. It is going to take months and maybe years to set up infrastructure in those territories", I said. "I can tell you that you will be missed in this city Mark", he said.

I awoke to someone knocking at the door. When I opened the door, it was my mom and Ralph. They were so excited as my mom sort of pushed her way in the door with Ralph tagging along. "What a beautiful home", my mom said. "I didn't get anything like this", Ralph said. My mom nearly runs to the bedroom. "Oh my, Ralph look at this", she said. Then she goes in the bathroom. "This is the biggest bathroom I have ever seen. I could spend a day in that bathtub and look at the shower Ralph", she said. You would have thought she had never been in a house before. "How long have you had this place?" she said. I have had it a while but have not been in it much", I said. "We are going out to dinner. You are coming", she demanded. "I guess I am. What's going on mom?" I asked as I smiled. "We will tell you in a minute. I am too excited to tell you right now", she said. We got in the Hover Car and flew to the Tower.

When we got to the table, Peter was right there asking us what we would like to drink. A few minutes later big Mike came out with a smile ear to ear. I have a meal made for a king. You must try it Mark. And of course the Governor and his lady are more than welcome to try it", he said. "Mike, this is my mom Marilyn", I said. "Now I see where you get your charm and looks Mark", Mike said. Mike was humming all the way back to the kitchen. "Ralph and I are going to be married", my mom spit out suddenly,. "I hope that is alright with you Mark", Ralph said. "I would be more than happy to have you as a dad Ralph. I hope that sounded right", I said. My mom put her arms around me and nearly pulled me from my chair. She was surely happy, I thought. Peter came with the food. It looked like a Chinese stir-fry with beef, shrimp and different vegetables and rice. We really enjoyed it. I have had nothing like this since I have been; my mind became suddenly confused by my different conscious sort of answering the questions different ways all at once. I probably had had nothing in my life, but I know my other life I did, I thought. I stay so confused all the time. I made a point to go into the kitchen and let Mike know how wonderful it tasted. Mike gave me a big hug. I guess I looked at my back to see if I had flour on my back. Mike said it was okay.

We left the dining facility and went up to the club. I guess we were going to celebrate now. The band had a guitar, cello, drummer and piano player. They did not sound bad. There were about 70 people in the club and few people were dancing. I will have to teach them some new songs, I thought to myself. Mom and Ralph were planning where they would go on their honeymoon. They were laughing and having fun like to children. Courtney came up to the table. "Do you think it is alright for me to have a few drinks here Mark?" she said. Ralph said, "sit down Courtney and join the celebration. I pulled a chair out for her. "Courtney, this is my mom Marilyn", I said. "Hi Mrs. Anglin", Courtney said. "You are such a beautiful young lady Courtney. You should get together with Mark", she said. "Courtney is my Executive Assistant mom", I said. "What happened to Dawn?" she asked. "She quit me", I said. "mmmm", she made a gesture. "We are celebrating our engagement tonight", my mom said. "You and the Governor?" Courtney asked. "Yes, yes, yes", she said with all smiles and giggles.

Cody from the band came over to the table. "Hi Mark, I was wondering if you might sing a few songs for us tonight?" he asked. "I would be happy to Cody", I said as I got up. "You two will have to dance this first song", I said. I walked across the floor with Cody. "Ladies and gentlemen, I would like to make an announcement. My mom Marilyn told me that she and Ralph

Namor were going to be married. Now, I know you don't know my mom, but most of you probably know Ralph Namor as the Governor of this fine city. Let's give them and great big hand as they get up and dance to this song." I played the piano and singing "From This Moment." Everyone seemed to hit the dance floor at once when I sang. I then sang "Unchained Melody." "Everyone, thank you for coming this evening and have a great time", I said. Everyone applauded as I went back to the table. Courtney said, "you sing beautiful Mark." "I don't think there is anything he can't do", Ralph said. Mom hugged my neck again real hard. "That song was so beautiful Mark, thank you, she said. Mom and Ralph got up for the next dance. I asked Courtney to dance. "Are you a pretty good dancer?" I asked. "I can keep up", she said. I got on the dance floor and that Fred Astaire dance mood hit me. I was all over the floor and Courtney stayed right with me. She was actually amazing. I was having the best time I have ever had dancing. People were applauding us dancing. We danced until about midnight, and then I took Courtney back to her apartment. Her apartment was right across from mine. "How did you get this apartment?" I asked. "The day I went to work; I told housing that I worked for you and they assigned me this flat", she said. I thanked her for a nice evening and I went over to my apartment. I sure was tempted to take her home with me. Everyone I knew was living close to me.

The next morning seemed to come too early. I was at the office by 7 AM. My cappuccino was waiting for me as usual. Courtney hugged me and told me she had a most wonderful time last night and let me know that the Directors were coming in. I went into the conference room to visit with them before the meeting. Sarah showed up with her cart and donuts. About a quarter to nine the Governor came in a sat down. George, the new security director came in last with a stern look on his face. "Let's get this meeting started. Mark get started; I know we have a lot to cover," the Governor said. "The first thing I need to say ladies and gentlemen is I don't know how many of you know that the United States attacked us. We intern sunk their carrier fleet, destroyed their air force and army. It was probably the shortest war in history. Even though you did not know what was going on, we could not have done it without your support. I will not get into the tangibles, but I would like to thank you. I am sorry we had to keep what we were doing secret. If we would have let out what we were doing, the spies that we had in our city and other cities would have reported and we probably could have lost cities and a lot of lives. As it was, we ended up destroying their capital city killing their president and cabinet along with over a million people that live in their capital city. That could have been us instead of them. We have a new Director George Stencil. For those that have not met him, please welcome him personally after the meeting. As for Mikella, she was fired because she gave out secret information. Even though she gave it to the President's staff, it was still secret. Secret means you do not tell your boss, your god if you are religious, you don't talk in your sleep or tell your dog because there is no one else to tell. Mikella is lucky that she was not terminated for treason. I need each and every one of you to understand that if you are told anything is a secret, it is just that a secret. Every other city in our country is getting the same speech", I said.

"Now I need everyone to work with me on the following. This is also going out to every city. As you know we took in more territories. Well, part of the peace treaty with the United States gave us more territories. We will break this nation up into states. Where we are will be called Texas. We will have New Mexico, Oklahoma, Arkansas, Colorado, Kansas, Missouri, Nebraska, Iowa, Minnesota, North and South Dakota. We will start in Minnesota first since it has a lot of natural resources that the corporation desperately needs right now. We need the resources to build cities and get the infrastructure set up in every state. The people in those states must be educated about how the corporate world works and the laws. I will need the following from you. I need 100 people from building. I need 50 contractors and 50 from the cubicle factory. The buildings in the other states will be built out of mostly plastic instead of cedar. They will also be heated and cooled. I will get with you on the specifics later John. I need 50 people from manufacturing. I will need 50 from security. Right now security has more than they need, so that should not be a problem. I will need fifty from science and technology, and 50 from health. I understand you are already short personnel Crystal, but we need to do our best in trying to recruit more nurses and doctors. Hopefully Betty can help with that. Betty, I am hoping we can get teachers in the states. If we can't get enough, then we may ask for volunteers. Services could probably be handled with local help. I will probably need a few people out of Human Resources and Housing to train people. I will probably need personnel from utilities. I am just not sure how many yet. Anyone volunteering to go to the territories must know that they will mostly be in a training capacity and will be gone for an indefinite time. All volunteers will be paid double pay or 120,000 credits whichever is more". I said.

The directors were mumbling back and forth to each other that many people would volunteer for double pay. "Who is going to guarantee the double pay", Sharon from HR said. "Some of you may or may not know that I have the authority in this country to authorize whatever I need to improve this country. You can verify with the Governor I have authority over all Governors in this country. Most of you know that whatever I have done here has been for the welfare of our citizens, our cities, and country. The Board Of Directors feel the same way and gave me the authority. Are there any other questions on that matter"? I asked. Everyone seemed to straighten up in their chairs. We went on discussing manpower and what each department and division would be responsible for. I let George know that security would be flying drones in the city. That will help him monitor what was going on.

I let them know that the dome and a small part of Boone city was hit by a jet and there was a loss of life and property damage. Those repairs should be done shortly and we will get full resources to finish up our dome. The new domes will be stronger and also will allow certain light filaments and air to enter allowing for plant growth in the city. We will also continue with construction of the New City on the east side. The cedar has come in. The new apartments, offices and businesses will have heating in the new flooring and cooling in the ceilings.

By next week we should have three new directors for services and one for building. HR has put out more ads for new personnel. We are also hoping the education program will help with getting more technical people and people for the university. We need people for nearly every department except security. We also have determined since the little war we had with the United States we might get some of their people to migrate here. We figured a lot of their people will tire of supporting the other half of their country. With their leadership disrupted, we figured they would probably have a lot of problems now and those problems will continue to increase. We will break for lunch and be back at 1:30PM to continue with any questions and answers. You might take a pad and pen to lunch and write down any ideas or comments you need to make or come up with. After lunch, I went over questions and answers that the directors wanted.

It took about three weeks to get all the volunteers ready and we loaded the planes to Minnesota. Planes and trucks with supplies to build the new city had already left. The new plastic sheeting with the burn inhibitor should protect city against any fires. The new system for building apartments, offices and businesses in the city is like putting an erector set together using nuts and bolts. Anyone following the instructions should be able to do it. That will make things a lot easier in areas where carpenters are not available. The first team going to Minnesota from all cities is over three thousand. I have the confidence we can swiftly build the cities and set up support and move to the next cities. I have so much I need to do. I just wish I knew what it all was. In any case, the next few years should be interesting.

TO BE CONTINUED: THE NEW FRONTIER

CPSIA information can be obtained
at www.ICGtesting.com
Printed in the USA
FSOW01n1925131217
41834FS